## Prologue

I looked into the gorgeous green eyes staring at me. This man was tall with dark hair fashionably cut and a hard jawline with a sexy five o'clock shadow. He was staring down at me as I sat tied to a chair in the middle of a penthouse kitchen. "At least he's hot," was all I could think. I wasn't scared like I should be. I didn't imagine I would die like this, but if I had to go at least I had some eye candy to look at. Deep down, I guess I had to know this was a possibility. Funny thing is, I wasn't sure how to feel. To know that you're the only good thing your father ever did in his life, felt big and oddly reassuring in my last moment. I wondered if my death would finally make my dad grow the hell up and be a decent person.

The man slowly started to stalk towards me. I locked my brown eyes with his green ones. I wanted him to see me and know that I would meet my death with my pride intact. I wanted him to see that I was nothing like the man who had a hand in making me. I was not a coward and if I had to pay the price for his lifestyle, I'd do it my way. The man slowed and stopped to stare. I wasn't begging for my life and I wouldn't. No one would mourn me, except maybe my dad and that was a hard maybe.

He started to come towards me again. I could see the knife in his hand. I wouldn't let him know that the sight of that did make me flinch on the inside. Death didn't scare me, but I wasn't a friend to pain. I hoped he did it quickly. I still uttered not a word. I kept my eyes locked with his and for some unknown reason, I smiled. I freaking smiled at him. He raised his hand with the knife, I stared, and....

## Chapter 1

"Smile!" My teacher said as she snapped a picture of me in my cap and gown.

It was sad that the whole town knew my own father wouldn't show for anything let alone give me money for a picture. I looked around and wasn't surprised to see I was solo for my graduation. My only family, my dad, Brian, wasn't even here to watch his only child and daughter graduate high school. I thought about the black, thinning haired greasy man I called my father and I sighed.

I tried not to feel jealous of all my classmates smiling with their families. I wished my mom was here. But, why should I. She left me with dad. I could almost understand. He never held down a job and gambled every dime we ever had. In fact, he was betting on horses at this very moment. I didn't have any friends either. How could I? I could barely afford to feed myself, let alone feed friends or afford to go to the mall or the movies.

I looked up to see Mr. Salinger, who I called Sal, waving at me smiling and coming towards me on the football field that we used for graduation. So, at least, I wasn't alone. Mr. Salinger was a man of about sixty. He was going bald and his hair that was left was completely gray. He was about six foot tall with a round belly and always wore Dickies coveralls and an old, dirty, feed store cap. He had a bushy mustache and always smiled. He had never been married or had any kids. He was a life saver for me.

I had worked at his little gas station/mechanic shop in our one stop light town from the time I was twelve. He hired me young, knowing I needed the money so I could feed myself and get clothes. I didn't work there on paper, but Sal always had cash for me at the end of the week and I was allowed to eat a hotdog and get a fountain drink while I was working. Mr. Salinger knew my father and what he didn't provide and felt bad for me when my mom left when I was only ten. Having the only gas station in town meant he heard everything.

Sal handed me an envelope. "Dee girl, happy graduation. This is for you. I'm proud of you girl. You've got a great work ethic and you've worked hard to get here."

Tears welled in my eyes and I hugged him. He was surprised. I never touched anyone. I wasn't a touchy person and liked my personal space. I wasn't nurtured or shown affection at home my whole life, so for me to show affection was hard. He patted my back.

"Thank you. Thank you. Thank you for being here. It seems that you're the only one who showed up for me." I said. I tried not to show the pain in my eyes.

I graduated with honors. I made all A's my high school career. I was getting out of my dad's house and making something of myself and I would never gamble my money off. I received a scholarship to the university that was three hours away. I was so ready to get out of there. My bags were packed. As soon as July 20th rolled around I would be gone.

"Dee let me give you a ride home. I'm sure you have some graduation party to get ready for tonight." He said winking at me.

I smiled and said, "I'd appreciate that, but you know I don't go to parties. I'm keeping my head clean for college. I've got too much to lose with a stupid decision."

He nodded and we walked to his 1965 Ford Shelby Cobra. It was bright blue with white racing stripes. That was his baby and he only brought her out on special occasions. Tears hit my eyes again. My own father couldn't make me feel special, but a man that owed me nothing was here for me to give me a ride in his fancy old car. I grabbed his arm and squeezed.

"Sal you brought Betty to give me a ride home. You just made my entire senior year special." I squealed.

I found a love for fast cars working at the gas station with him. He taught me a lot too. I could work on cars with the best of men. I had my eye on a 1978 Pontiac Firebird Trans Am. She wasn't the prettiest girl and needed some help to get going, but I knew I could get her to run and give her a facelift with some paint. She had T-tops and I could just imagine my hair blowing in the wind while I drove her hard and fast.

We got in his car and told me, "Open your envelope."

I did and a title fell out into my lap. It was for my Firebird. I jumped in the seat with excitement and threw my arms around his neck again. "I can't believe you got her for me. This is too much. I can't accept this." I said earnestly to him.

"Nonsense it's my gift to you. I never had children and Dee, you're the closest thing I have. I want to give that to you and plus I got a great deal on it. She doesn't run, so you have some work to do before you leave for school so you have some wheels." Sal said looking right into my soul.

I did cry now. "I wish you were my dad. You taught me more than my actual father. I can change my own oil or a flat if I get one and I can fix my own motor if need be. You gave me work and purpose when I needed it and I know you paid me too much at times. Without you, I don't what would have happened to me. Thank you. I will fix her up and make you proud." I promised.

"I know you will. You already do. What are you going to name her?" He asked with his bushy eyebrows raised.

"Fiona. Fiona the fast Firebird. I think I should paint her sparkly purple or maybe green." I said getting excited thinking of all the possibilities.

Mr. Salinger smiled at me. I could see a wave of emotion in him too. We had spent many Christmases together over the years. My dad would leave at the drop of a hat for some bet or sometimes leave me on his doorstep, because some bookie was looking for him to pay up. Most years the only Christmas presents I would get would be from Sal. He bought me my own set of tools for his shop the first Christmas I was working for him. He made me feel better about accepting them by saying he was going to teach me how to use them and it was more of an investment for him to have a decent worker there.

On my fifteenth birthday, he put me in driver's ed. He said that he did that so I could drive to pick up parts for him. He always tried to make his gifts for me seem like they were benefiting him so I wouldn't feel bad. On my sixteenth birthday, he let me drive Betty. He even took a picture of me in the driver's seat and framed it and put it up in his office. I smiled remembering the memories.

"Thank you. For. Everything. I really do love ya." I told him.

"It's been my pleasure to watch you grow and learn and right back at ya Dee girl." He told me.

I hugged him one more time after he put Betty in park in front of the shabby two bedroom, one bath, house I slept in with my father when he was home. I got out and went and unlocked the door and sighed as I shut it behind me. I quietly let the tears fall.

Chapter 2

I looked around the sparse house. It had a single arm chair in the living room and one floor lamp. It really was a poor excuse of a home. There was no TV and the cringey, floral wall paper was starting to come off in random places. Another of the many reasons I didn't have friends. I could never bring them back here. I walked to my small bedroom. It was the best room in the house. I had a patchwork quilt on my bed and blue shaggy curtains. I had a bookshelf, filled with old, vintage books. Not having money will make you resourceful. I found out at a young age that I could escape in a good book.

Everything I owned was second hand. I didn't have much money, but I learned how to live on little to nothing. All my school clothes, books, room décor, I bought at resale shops. I appreciated everything I had too. I would be a decent, productive human being. I knew what I didn't want to be. My only hope was that when I made something of myself, my dad wouldn't be on my doorstep with his hands out waiting for me to take care of his screwups.

I had paid one of his debts before. A scary looking guy was waiting on the doorstep to the house one night as I got home from the gas station. He looked surprised to see a brown headed, girl coming in on a bicycle covered in grease. He looked awful when he realized I was the daughter to the creep that owed his boss money.

"Brian is your dad?" He had asked in a burly, deep voice.

I had nowhere to run, so I just went with honesty. I had said, "Yes sir. What has he done now?"

"He owes my boss some money and I'm here to get it. Kid, why don't you go somewhere else and we pretend we didn't see each other. I don't want to have to say I saw you." The big man really was trying to do me a favor.

The problem was I had nowhere to go. Mr. Salinger was gone for the weekend. I was alone. "Sir, I have nowhere else to go. I just got home from work and my boss has left for out of town. Are you going to hurt me or something? I'd really prefer you didn't." I said in an even tone. Any normal young girl would not be rational at this moment. She would be terrified out of her mind.

"Wait you work? You can't be more than what thirteen? Kid you are a tough one. I don't like to hurt kids, but some of the other guys your dad gets caught up with aren't as nice. I have to take my boss something sweetheart. Do you know if your dad has anything of value in your house. A watch? Anything?" The big guy asked.

I looked down at my feet. I took a deep breath and asked, "How much does he owe?"

The big man looked at me and I saw a flash of something. Regret maybe or sadness? "He has to give him at least $1000.00 now."

I nodded my little head. "Well you might as well come in." I told the big guy.

He followed me inside and I could see he was shocked to see the little bit of nothing in the house. He looked to me with a knowing look and sighed. He followed me to my room and watched as I pulled a plant out of a pot in my windowsill. Under the plant, I had a roll of money I had been saving for school clothes. I saved most of my cash, but only spent what I needed to on food. I could tell he felt awful. I started to count my money. I only had $724.

I looked up to the big guy and told him, "This is all I have. This is everything I've saved for a year and a half. Will this work to keep me safe? I don't want to be collateral damage for my father's bad choices. I'm not like him."

The big man studied me, "I can make this work sweetheart. I'm sorry to have to take your hard work. I'm not lying kid when I say that. I really wish I didn't have to take your money and I promise not let anyone know that your dad has a kid. But look, you won't always be safe with the guys your dad plays around with. Is there anywhere you can go kid?"

I just shook my head no. I had no one. He looked at me and made an apologetic face. He left that night and told me to always pay attention and never to stop in my driveway again if someone was there, because not everyone liked kids like he did. I found out he had a daughter too. He told me to keep working hard and I could get myself out of there one day. I found it funny that he was telling me that knowing that he did some guy's dirty work, but I guess he got paid well.

A week later my dad showed up. He was on one of his highs. He had actually won somewhere, but I knew better than to be happy. Eventually he lost it all again. He came in with pizza and sodas. "Hey Dee. Your dad did it this time. My numbers hit big. Come get some pizza." He hollered.

I came out. I grabbed a slice and thanked him. He looked at me a long while and then asked, "Where did you get a thousand dollars?"

I looked confused. Then it hit me. The big scary guy. He wasn't concerned that some guy had come into our house or that I was confronted with dealing with his debt and could have been hurt. He was worried about where I got the money.

"I didn't have a thousand. I only had seven hundred and you know I work. I've been saving for school clothes." I explained.

He looked at me funny. "That's weird. A guy called me and said my daughter had paid a thousand bucks on my debt for me."

I shrugged my shoulders. I assumed he must've paid the rest with his winnings and then I realized that the big guy must have spotted me the rest of the money. Even big, scary guys have hearts. I said a silent thank you to him.

Life was good for two weeks, but I never got my money back from him. That was no surprise. He always had this crazy idea that I owed him for having a place to live and not to mention giving me life. He had such a warped sense of what he deserved. In two weeks, he lost everything again betting on basketball games. Him coming home in a new car to have it disappear the next week was normal.

I shook my head trying to come back to reality. I walked to my mirror on my closet door. I looked at myself in my cap in gown. I was slender, with a nice round butt, and full breast. I guess the pear shape. I looked like my mother. I had dark brown hair and brown eyes. I had a nice mouth with pretty teeth. I wondered if she even thought about me. She had just left and never looked back. I could understand wanting to leave dad. But why did she leave me? She had to know what I would be facing.

I tried to ignore the ache inside me. My father didn't love me enough to even do the basic things a parent should: keep me safe, fed, and clothed. My mother just left me there with him when I was not old enough to care for myself. I had a terrible feeling that I could never be loved. My father never said it. I knew Mr. Salinger loved me in his own way, but I mean really loved. He never forgot my birthday or let a Christmas go by without a gift. He managed to give me what I needed without it feeling like a handout. I wanted someone to love me more than themselves and put me first for once. It seemed like an unreachable dream. I was too embarrassed to date. I could never introduce them to my father, much less bring them home. I had no real nice clothes to wear. I had never even been kissed. Man my life was really screwed up. What eighteen year old girl alive was there that had never even been kissed?

Chapter 3

I threw my cap and gown off and laid out on my bed. I would miss Mr. Salinger when I left, but I couldn't wait to start somewhere fresh. Somewhere that no one knew me and I wouldn't be the poor girl with a screw up father. Somewhere that I would just be Dee, the smart girl, who is nice, and loves fast cars. I wanted a real family so badly. I wanted to be loved and maybe even touched.

Ring! Ring! My house phone rang. Yes, house phone. My poor butt couldn't afford a cell, so I still had a land line. I jumped startled. The only person to call here was Mr. Salinger or sometimes the school.

"Hello?" I answered.

"I may have to wrong the number. I apologize ma'am," said a really nice, rich, deep voice.

"Oh. Ok. No problem." I said. "Have a good evening."

"This isn't by chance a Brian's house?" The nice sounding man asked.

My heart sank to my stomach. Who got my phone number and how did they know to call it? How deep was he in now?

"No. I'm afraid this is my number. Have a great eve…" I was cut off.

"Ma'am, I need to know if Brian is there," said the guy in a completely calm manner.

"Look, that piece of shit is my father. I don't know where he is. I have no clue what he's gotten himself into now, but please, leave me out of it. I just graduated literally two hours ago. He didn't even show for that, so you think he would care who's calling my number? I'll answer for you, no. He doesn't give a shit about me. Please just leave me alone. I'm almost done here. I'll be getting out of her soon. I really am sorry for whatever he did, but seriously, I don't know where he is or when he'll be back." I spewed from my mouth. I don't know what came over me, but I just let it all fly. I knew I had just screwed up. You can't ever tell anyone you even know him. Had I just made myself a target?

There was a pause on the line and then the man spoke again, "I see. I'm sorry. Congratulations on your graduation. I'm sorry to bother your evening. I'm sure you're celebrating."

"Oh yes celebrating big with the only family I have gone somewhere surely betting his last dime on something he'll never win." I sighed. What the hell, he already knows.

"Look, I'm sorry. Pretend I never called. I'll get to your uh, dad, another way. Goodnight." The tantalizing voice said through my phone.

Click. Silence. I flung myself back down on my bed and sighed heavily. Great, one of my dad's bookie goons was calling my number looking for him now. At least he said congratulations. I laughed madly at the thought. Maybe I could get out of here soon. I double checked to make sure both doors were locked. The call had me uneasy. If he knew my land line number, I'm sure he knew my address. I went to my bed and tried to get sleep.

The next morning, I got up with the sun. I needed out of the house. I hid my Firebird Title. That was something I knew better than to let my dad find. That would be his next bet collateral if he found it. The man had been stealing anything of value from me since I could remember. Anything worth a dime would be used to make his next gamble. I needed to go get my hands working and mind moving on to something else. I was going to work on Fiona. When I stepped out of the house, in my old jeans with holes and a white T-shirt with my long hair in a ponytail, I felt like I could feel someone watching me. You know that creepy feeling that eyes are on you. I had that. I looked around and didn't see anyone.

I had learned from the big, scary guy to always keep my eyes open and observe everything around me. I took the time to scan across the road and all around me. Nothing. Weird. Maybe I was still freaked out over the phone call last night. I had slipped. I should've never said that Brian was my father. No one needed to know that. I got on my bicycle, yes bicycle. That's all I had until yesterday. I rode it slowly, taking in the sunshine with my face raised up to the sky to get to the gas station/mechanic shop. I loved the way the sun felt on my skin. I wished I could lounge by a pool somewhere. That was a goal of mine, to live somewhere with a pool I could lay by whenever I wanted to.

The eerie feeling someone was watching me never left me. I got to the station and hollered hi to Sally, Mr. Salinger's counter clerk. Sally was about forty and round and the sweetest lady ever. He hired her when I turned fifteen, because I was more help to him in the mechanic shop. I walked into the bays to see he already had Fiona in the last one for me. He rolled out from under a Z71 he was working on. U Joints I was guessing.

"There's my girl. I knew you would be coming in on your day off to get started. She's over there for you. You can use any parts I have on hand here to fix her and make a list of what you need that we don't have," said Mr. Salinger with a knowing smile on his face.

He truly probably did know me better than anyone else.  Sal was the only constant in my life and worth more than gold to me. In all honesty, he was the only family I had. He was looking around for something. I grabbed his wrench and rag before he even asked. I probably knew him better than anyone else too. He winked at me and I smiled and mouthed, "Thank you."

I walked over to the last bay and flung the big door open to let the sunshine and air in. As I opened the door I held on to it and let I stretch my body out. I needed my body stretched and my mind calm so I could focus on Fiona. As the door came to a stop at the top, I looked around outside. I noticed an orange Dodge Charger parked across the street. I nodded my approval of it. I turned and faced Fiona and walked around her, one finger tracing my path across her as I went. I didn't notice the guy in the Charger watching me. I was caught in my car haze.

I also didn't notice when he got out of the car to walk into the gas station to buy a cherry coke and a candy bar. My head was under her hood, checking spark plugs and anything else that I could easily fix with stuff on hand. I didn't feel his eyes on me when I went under her to check the undercarriage. She definitely needed fresh oil and a filter. The brakes were not too great either, but it was all fixable. She needed a new starter too. I came out from under her and that's when I felt like I was being watched again. It was totally nothing out of the ordinary at work. People always seemed shocked to see a young woman working on cars.

"Hey Sal!" I hollered at Mr. Salinger.

He looked up to me from under the truck with his eyebrows raised in question.

"I'm going to get me a cherry coke and Tootsie pop. You want anything old man?" I teased.

He smiled and shook his head no. He was in the zone and wouldn't be back out from under that truck until it was fixed. I knew that look.

I washed my hands at the oil stained work sink before walking into the side door of the gas station store. A handsome man was at the counter checking out. He looked at me as I walked in. I gave him a smile. My smile was probably the nicest thing I had. I used it often, especially on Sal's customers. He returned a crooked smile. I figured he must have been the one watching the girl working on an old car. Behind Sally's counter was big windows that were open to the shop. You could watch your vehicle get worked on from the store side.

I went to the fountain drinks and got me a cherry coke and then went up to the counter and leaned over and grabbed me a tootsie pop from my stash of cherry flavored ones. Needless to say, my favorite flavor was cherry. The handsome man was still up there, openly staring at me. I stared back for a moment.

Sally broke our stare, "I didn't get to tell you congratulations when you walked in Dee. You were too quick getting to your new baby." She smiled.

"Oh thanks Sally. I was excited to get to work on Fiona." I replied.

The handsome guy raised an eyebrow and I noticed he had gorgeous emerald green eyes. "Fiona?" He asked.

I laughed and said, "Yes Fiona. That's my Firebird's name. Doesn't everyone name their cars?"

His mouth quirked again and he said, "Tammy."

I looked at him in his eyes now and smiled.

"My Charger is named Tammy." He laughed out. "I've never told anyone that."

I smiled even bigger. "Tammy's a nice name. A safe name." I teased.

He smiled even bigger at me too. "Tammy is a fine name for a fine car."

"Well you heard Sally call me Dee. So what's your name?" I asked the handsome, green eyed man.

He raised an eyebrow and smiled, "Trent. Nice to meet you Dee."

"Nice to meet you Trent." I responded trying his name out on my tongue.

"Miss. Sally I'd like to pay for her drink and candy too with mine please," said Trent.

"Oh honey, those suckers are Dee's. She keeps a stash of nothing but cherry ones back here and gives all the other flavors to any kids that come through here. And she gets her drinks for free here. Ol' Sal loves his best mechanic besides him here." Sally laughed.

Trent was pleasantly surprise. He asked, "The best mechanic eh? Only cherry suckers?"

"Yep the only flavor worth enjoying along with my cherry coke," I said holding up my drink towards him and ignoring the best mechanic thing.

"That's what I get too," said Trent holding up his drink.

I opened my Tootsie Pop and stuck it in mouth and pulled it out. Trent's eyes glazed over. I totally didn't mean it in a suggestive manner. "Well, I got to get back to Fiona. I think I could have her up and running in a couple weeks. It was pleasure Trent." I said turning to walk off.

"I hope to see you around Dee," said to Trent to my back as I got to the side door.

I just turned my head, smiled, and gave him a slight nod.

I got back to Fiona and kept my sucker in my mouth as I worked on her and thought it all through.  She needed new tires. I grabbed a pen and paper and made my list. I had done all I could do on her for the day, so I got a rag and started wiping her down. I was singing to myself and dancing silly as I wiped her down.

"Dee!" Sal hollered.

I looked up to see what Sal needed.

"Would you mind changing the oil on that Charger for me. I know it's your day off, but I'm almost done with this one," said Sal.

"Of course! I'm here anyway and I always like getting my hands on a fine car." I hollered back. I heard a chuckle from beside the car. I looked over to see Trent there. So Tammy was the sexy, orange, Charger.

I moved to bay two and motioned for Trent to pull in. He got in his car and did. I could hear the turbo in it. She sounded fast. My eyes lit as she loped into the garage. I had car lust. I motioned for him to stop. I told him she sounded nice and his eyes lit up. I told him he could wait inside if he wanted, but he said he preferred to sit in his car. I nodded and got to work.

When he popped the hood, my eyes bulged out. That engine was and orgasm on wheels, not that I knew what orgasm actually felt like, but this had to be close. I smiled at him. "Tammy's sexy." I told him smiling.

He smiled back. He knew.

I quickly got to work. I popped another sucker in my mouth and went under her. Her undercarriage was just as nice. You could tell he took good care of her. I was curious as to why he decided to get his oil changed here in our little po-dunk place. Maybe he had a long way to travel. He was clearly not from our small town. I didn't recognize him. I could feel him watching me as I worked. When I finished the oil and the filter, I was a little dirty. I had an oil splat on my shirt.

"Looks like I owe you a new shirt," said Trent.

"Oh no. Hazard of the job. This is a work shirt anyhow." I said grabbing the window washer.

I plunged the window squeegee in the bucket and started to wipe down his windshield. I felt air on my skin as the bottom of my shirt raised a little to expose the bottom part of my stomach as I stretched across to wipe his window. I shifted the sucker in my mouth to my cheek as I fought back a blush. I looked in the windshield to see he was watching me and noticed his eyes trail to the exposed skin at my stomach. I quickly looked the other way and finished up the job.

"Ok Sal. This one is all finished up." I hollered not making eye contact with Trent.

"Ok be right there Dee," said Sal.

I pulled the sucker out of my mouth and turned to walk away.

"Thank you for taking care of Tammy, Dee," said Trent.

I smiled and nodded and kept walking away. I didn't turn back around. I was too nervous to. It was much easier to work on a car and not have to talk to anyone. I kept thinking man Trent was handsome, but he had to be at least twenty five and I was just barely eighteen and I had college to go off to and I needed to figure out how to live. But my gosh, he had to be the best looking man I had ever seen and he liked cherry cokes and fast cars. I had never been intimate at all and I wasn't sure if I wanted to be touched or not touched more. I shook my head and walked back into the store side.

"That guy was making eyes at you." Sally said smiling at me.

"No. I'm sure not. He's probably just surprised to see a chick working on cars like everyone else." I said back sighing, somewhat wishing that perhaps maybe someone really saw me.

"Hun, I know what kind of look he was giving you and was the kind that says he wanted to taste you!" She giggled.

I busted out laughing! "Sally you're not right!"

"See you tomorrow pretty girl!" She hollered as I walked out to get on my bike.

Chapter 4

I rode all the way home smiling. Even if nothing would ever come about Trent, it was nice to be noticed. Maybe Sally was right and he did think something of me. I walked away though. You shouldn't make it easy for them to catch you. I'd be leaving for school in a month. I took in the sun on my way home. I closed my eyes and let my mind wander to a better life that I would make for myself one day.

I turned into our holey driveway and sighed. This was not the life I wanted. I was ready to get out. As I sat my bike up against the house, the feeling I was being watched prickled against my skin again. I looked all around again for the second time today. I didn't see anyone. Gosh my mind got the best of me sometimes. But seriously, who wouldn't be paranoid twenty-four-seven not knowing who would be looking for your dad next. I shook my head and unlocked my busted up door and walked inside.

The air always seemed to leave me as I walked into the house. It may not have been a prison cell, but it didn't feel nice either. My dad had never laid a hand on me, never called me anything ugly, he just never did anything towards me at all. He barely acknowledged my existence. He was MIA more than he was home. He never spoke a soft or encouraging word to me. I felt alone in this place. Isolated. I had no friends, no love. Sure I had Sal, but I was missing so much.

I went to the poor excuse of a kitchen and got a bowl. Cereal for dinner. What a life. I sat alone at the tiny breakfast table with two mismatched chairs. I put my hands in my head and let out a silent scream. Then, I thought of Fiona. I had a purpose. Something to fix up and get going so I could get going.

The next weeks passed all about the same. I got up, got to work, and worked on Fiona. Sally teased me about Trent wanting to know if I saw him again. I told her no. I didn't give him my number or anything. Plus how embarrassing would it be to tell him, "If I don't answer you'll just have to call again later. I can't afford a cell phone." No. I would rather him think I was pretty and mysterious and could fix a car up.

I still would get the sense every now and then someone was watching me, but I let it go. My dad still hadn't appeared back home and it had been over a month. I often wondered when I would get the police knocking at the door to tell me they found him in the bottom of a lake somewhere with cement blocks on his feet. Seriously that shit should only happen in movies, but it seemed to be part of his life for real and in consequence mine too.

A week before it was time for me to leave, I sat behind the wheel of my Fiona. I took a deep breath, put a foot on the brake and the other on the clutch, and turned the key in the ignition. She roared to life! I let out a happy whoop. I looked over to see Sal smiling at me.

"Sal come hop in! You have to be with me on her first ride!" I hollered smiling ear to ear.

He didn't hesitate. He threw his blue rag down and jumped in. I slowly backed her out of the last bay, feeling the motor lope beneath me. I had her fixed up and she had a whopping 215 horsepower working under that beautiful hood. She was a four speed manual and she purred to be driven hard. I got her turned around and put my foot on the clutch, put her in first, and gave her a little gas. She was alive and moving. I got her out on an old back road and was shifting gears like it was second nature. I laughed as she showed me what she had. Sal was laughing too. I pulled over to the side of the road and got out.

"Dee girl whatcha doing?" Sal questioned me.

"You let me drive Betty and you gave me Fiona. I think it's only fair you drive her back to the shop." I said smiling at him and opening his door.

Sal smiled so big that his cheeks had to hurt. He got out and went to the driver's side and let out a laugh. He put her in gear and drove her hard. We made it back to the shop and he was praising my hard work. "Now Dee girl, have you decided what color you're going to paint her? You only have week before you leave me for college," said Sal.

"I'm thinking I'd like to see her a nice glittery forest green. I want it to say classy and flashy." I said beaming.

He liked it. He nodded. "The paint will be in two days. So you better start sanding and priming her for her paint."

I saluted him and moved Fiona to the very back garage. It was a garage separate all on its own. It's where we painted. You had to be away from all the other cars and somewhere with good ventilation. I parked Fiona and got out. I ran my hand down her side. "We will make some good memories." I told the car. I started working her, grinding off all the old paint and buffing out a couple dents. Tomorrow I would prime her after we closed the mechanic shop. I couldn't abandon Sal to work alone all day.

The next day, I worked my tail off with Sal fixing cars and changing oil. When five rolled around, I headed out to the back garage. I put on an airbreather so I wouldn't inhale too much of the fumes from the primer and got to work after making sure all my windows where covered and taped well. I finished up and looked at her. "Don't worry Fiona. This is just the base. You're real make up will be here in the morning and we will get you shined up like a new penny."

I rode my bike home in the dark. I didn't particularly like riding home at night, but Fiona was top priority. I had to have her done by the next week. I would be leaving for college. When I pulled into the bumpy drive, I notice the living room light on. There was no car in the driveway, so it must be dad. He lost it all again and has come crawling home.

"Dad," I said as I opened the unlocked door.

Nothing.

I walked in and looked around. It was quiet. Too quiet. I walked to my dad's room and noticed his drawers were all wide open and all of his clothes were gone. It looked like he left in a hurry. "Shit. Dad what have you got yourself into now?" I wondered aloud.

I made it to my room to find it had been destroyed too. My bed was overturned. My books were all out the shelves and a few of my older ones were missing. That jerk had stolen my books to pawn for money.

It wasn't the first time he had taken my things to see what he could get for them. I looked in my windowsill. My plant was still there like nothing had happened. I smiled to myself. He never thought to check that plant. I went to it and pulled the plant up to find the false bottom where I kept my roll of saved cash and now my car title.

My eyes wondered around my room. I was ready to leave. I wondered if I was safe. On graduation night a man had called looking for him and now all the sudden all of my dad's clothes are missing. I called Sal. I was scared to stay home. I had learned to trust my gut.

"Hello. This is Sal." He answered.

"Hey Sal. I'm sorry to bother you so late. I just..I...can I come crash at your place?" I asked.

I heard Sal's voice change and the worry hit it as he said, "I'm coming to get you. Bring everything you have packed with you. You just stay with me until it's time to leave for school. Okay?"

"Okay." I whispered trying to hold back the tears.

Sal was at my house in ten minutes. He didn't knock. He got out of his car and came right in. He walked past my dad's room to see his clothes all gone and came straight to my room. He inhaled deeply when he saw all my things thrown about.

"Did your dad steal your stuff?" He asked turning red with anger.

"Just some books. He didn't find my cash stash or Fiona's title. I'm ok. I'm just freaked out that he took all his clothes. I don't feel safe here right now. Anyone could have followed him." I said looking around one last time.

Sal grabbed my only suitcase and I grabbed my backpack, another bag, and my plant. We went to his car and loaded everything up. Sal lived in a small two bedroom house right by his shop. I always had a room there. He even had tried to get me to move in at one time, but Sal was a lifelong bachelor and I wouldn't do that to him. I told him knowing that he was there for me and I had a place when need be was more than enough and it was true. Plus my dad would have never allowed that, because I was a nice tax bonus for him. Guess I wouldn't matter now that he wouldn't  be getting his child bonus at tax time.

"Sal thank you. I don't know where I would be without you. You are the closest thing I have to a dad and I just want you to know you mean a lot to me," I said letting the tears fall silently.

Sal wrapped me up in a bear hug and said, "I know Dee girl. I love you like you're my own and I'll never understand how your dad can do what he does to you. You are special and smart and capable of anything. Don't let anyone tell you otherwise. It takes more than blood to be a dad and I'm honored to step up for you Dee girl. Get some rest. You got a car to paint in the morning."

I took a shaky breath and nodded and kissed his cheek. Sal was like my own personal guardian angel. He had to know how much he meant to me.

Chapter 5

I woke up in my bed at Sal's excited. My room there had muscle car posters all over the walls and my twin bed had a Jeff Gordon throw on it. Sal was a bachelor, but I loved cars so it was perfect. Today was the day Fiona would get her paint. I went to the kitchen and started the coffee and rummaged Sal's fridge to see what I could make us for breakfast. I ended up making bacon, cheese, bell pepper, and onion omelets. Sal loved when I stayed because I enjoyed cooking and he always had more food than me.

"You're going to make someone a good wife one day Dee." He said after taking a big bite of his omelet.

"I don't even know if I want to get married Sal. I think I would like kids someday though. I don't know. That all seems scary to me." I said.

"Good thing you don't have to figure it all out now, but I wouldn't mind being Papa Sal. Just saying. But go live life, make some mistakes, fall in love, and if you find someone worthy of you, which I will say no one will ever be good enough, but if he's worthy of you, see what happens." Sal said seeming to be off somewhere else.

"Are you talking from experience my never married, no kid, business owning, boss man?" I teased.

He looked at me knowingly, "I do have a kid. You. But yes from experience. There are times that I wish I had settled down and married my high school sweetheart. It's not always easy to be alone and it's not always easy to be vulnerable to someone. Sometimes it's hard to see the person we need right in front of us. Now don't get me wrong. I've had a lot of fun. But fun if it's meaningless is just that, meaningless. But live life Dee. You get what I'm saying?"

"I'm not going to go off to college to get meaningless fun. Is that what you're worried about and I think I'm hearing you say not to have any regrets, but not to be afraid to fall for someone. Am I reading between the lines correctly?" I asked

He just nodded.

I had never had the sex talk with anyone and poor Sal was doing his best. I heard enough at school and knew it was something serious. There would be no way I'd ever chance bringing another life into my mine when it was so screwed up and I wanted to make sure I chose the right guy and not end up like my own mother.

"I love ya Sal," I said smiling at him. He cared for me so much.

"Love ya too Dee girl and I'm proud of you and can't wait to see where life takes you," Sal replied.

We finished our breakfast in silence and then made our way to the shop. I felt so at peace with Sal. We both said some things the other needed to hear. I was glad I told him how much he meant to me before I left for college. I would come back of course to help him when I could.

"You just go paint your Fiona today. I have a light day in the shop. Oh and one more thing," he said pulling something out of his pocket. "I got you this so we can keep in touch when you're off at school shining."

It was a cell phone in a sparkly green case. I took it with a shaky hand and looked at it and then looked at Sal with a soft expression on my face. I did know love. Sal showed me love.

"Thank you." I whispered.

He patted my shoulder and said, "Go get to work."

I laughed and headed to the garage.

I put on my mask and got to work. I blared old rock music as I painted my Fiona forest green. She was coming to life. I kept feeling like someone was peeking in. I figured it was Sal checking on me and my progress, so I didn't bother to look up. At eight O'clock in the evening I was done. She had two coats and her clear coat on. I made Sal come in and help me take the tape and coverings off her windows and lights. She looked gorgeous. I smiled at Sal.

"Sally is still here. Drive Fiona up in front of the bay doors and let's get a picture!" Sal said excitedly.

When Sal was that excited, you just did what he asked. I drove her up there and Sal and Sally were waiting with the camera. I handed Sally my new cell phone and asked her to snap a couple pictures on there too. Sal came over and put an arm around me and smiled like the proud father he truly was to me. We did some silly poses too and then Sal wanted one of just me for his wall. He grabbed his camera from Sally and said, "Say cheese Dee girl!"

I did and he started snapping pictures and then it happened. He grabbed his chest and fell to the ground. I cried out! "Sal!"

Sally already had her phone out dialing 911. "We need an ambulance over at Sal's shop now! He grabbed his chest and fell over. Yes he's breathing. No I don't think so. No he hasn't. Heart attack? Please hurry."

Everything was a blur to me. I held Sal in my arms and kept telling, "Get your ass up Sal. What are you doing? Sal. Sal!"

When the paramedics got there, they had to pry me off of Sal. I got in the ambulance with them. They asked me, "Ma'am who are you?"

I replied, "His daughter." Because I was. In that moment. I realized what I had known most of my life, he was my dad.

They didn't question me and they let me ride with him. I held his hand and watched them work. They hooked him up to an IV and were checking all his vitals. His heart wasn't beating correctly. He was in fact having a heart attack. The paramedics looked at one another. I could tell there was something bad in their unspoken expressions.

One of them spoke gently to me, "He's having a major heart attack. We are doing our best, but I'm not sure we will even make it to the hospital. Just let him know you're here. Talk to him."

I nodded and let the tears fall. "Sal. I'm here and I'm not leaving you. Wake your stubborn ass up and get your heart to beat right. I need you. I always have. I love you Sal. A girl couldn't ask for a better dad." I said putting his hand to my tear streaked cheek.

His thumb rubbed at the tears. His eyes were still closed and his face looked in pain. He wasn't even coherent moments before and now he was rubbing my cheek.

"Sal," I whispered, "I love you Dad."

Sal opened his eyes and turned to my tear soaked face and whispered, "And I love you my Dee girl. You were the biggest joy of my life."

"Don't talk like you're leaving me. You can't leave me too. I need you." I cried in racked sobs.

He continued to rub my cheek and whispered, "Sometimes the choice isn't ours on when we leave. Just know that I would never leave you if I had the chance to do otherwise. My biggest accomplishment was seeing you fix up Fiona on your own. You can make it in this world Dee girl. You will be fine and never doubt for a moment that I love you."

The beeping on the machines started to go haywire. Something was wrong. The paramedics said something about cardiac arrest and pulled me aside, but I never let go of Sal's hand. I squeezed it trying to will my heart to beat for his, but in the end it wasn't enough. He turned his head and looked at me one final time and even gave a small smile. I just mouthed I love you and then he let go and I was once again all alone in this dark world.

Sally had been following the ambulance and when we got to the hospital I ran out and ran straight to her. She caught me up in a hug and sank to the ground with me. Sally knew what Sal and I meant to each other and hell Sally loved him too. Sal had a way of taking care of the people in his life. I cried on the ground in the parking lot for what seemed like hours and Sally just held me. She asked me if I wanted to go home with her, but I said no. I needed to go back to Sal's, because all my things were there and Fiona was still up front. So, Sally dropped me off with a final squeeze on my hand.

I got in Fiona and started her up and drove her back to paint garage. I sat in her for a long time with my head on the steering wheel. How could my life be so messed up that the only person who really loved me be gone? My head was pounding from all the crying. I took a deep ragged breath and stepped out of my beautiful, green Firebird.

"Dee." I heard a deep man's voice say my name and I spun around.

Chapter 6

My eyes went wide, as I recognized the handsome, green eyed man standing in the paint garage. "Trent? What are you doing here?" I questioned, not trying to sound scared out of my mind.

"I need you to come with me right now," said Trent looking straight at me.

"Um. No. I don't really know you and I have to be here. There's a lot going on." I said firmly.

"Fiona looks real good. You did a good job." He said approvingly.

"Yeah. Thanks. But why are you here?" I asked again.

"Dee. I don't think you understand. You are coming with me." Trent said cool as ice.

"No. I'm not. Get out of here now." I said raising my voice.

Trent started to walk towards and I started to back away. I had a screwdriver just on the other side of Fiona. "You need to leave now!" I shouted.

"Not without you Dee. You don't understand what's going on here. I don't have a choice and neither do you." He said.

"You always have a choice." I spat out as I grabbed the screwdriver.

Trent noticed I had grabbed it. His eyes went narrow. "So I see we will have to do this the hard way."

"What the hell Trent? I took good care of Tammy and we both like cherry coke and I was nice to you. Just because we have a few things in common and you have gorgeous eyes and I was nice to you, doesn't mean we are going to be close friends." I said gripping the screwdriver hard, ready to pounce.

His eyes warmed. Yes freaking warmed. And then he did it. He pulled a gun out. A black Glock. He aimed it straight at my head. My head wasn't working right. I felt like I had nothing to lose. Sal was gone. My father was an idiot. My mother left me and I was at the end of my damn rope. I didn't care that he was holding a gun. I ran at him and hit him in the head with the butt of the screwdriver.

"You think death scares me you idiot? I have nothing to lose. Sal died. I have no one. I'm alone. So joke's on you if you kill me. I won't be a headliner to make you famous, because literally no one cares about me now." I screamed as I hit him again and again.

"Damn it Dee. Stop! This isn't what I want." He hollered as I went crazy on him. I couldn't imagine why he just hadn't shot me yet. I felt a thud on my head. Then, my world went black.

Chapter 7

I woke up moaning. My head was beating. This was the worst headache I had ever had. I went to reach up to put my hands on my head to realize they were tied. Shit. What had happened? That's right. Trent. He had a gun, but didn't shoot me. I had attacked him and he must have hit me over the head with his hand gun. I felt us moving. We were in a car. I hadn't opened my eyes yet. I was afraid to.

"Dee, I know you're awake. I can see your eyes twitching under your lids and I saw you try to move your hands to your head." He said from next to me.

I opened my eyes and was immediately pissed. We were in Fiona and he was driving her. "You freaking asshole! You are touching Fiona. You don't deserve to touch her, let alone drive her. You are a car rapist!" I hollered, realizing how hilarious it sounded after I said it and I started to laugh hysterically.

Trent looked a little worried at my outburst and then he started to laugh too. "Car rapist? Really? I held you at gun point, knocked you over the head, and tied you up and you're worried about me driving Fiona?"

"You don't get to say her name and yes I'm pissed. Fiona is mine. I worked so hard on her. But ok I'll ask...Why the hell did you kidnap me?" I asked staying angry.

"Well, that's the problem. I've been watching you a while. I didn't mean to stumble across you in all honestly, but I did which leads us here. Brian, your father, owes my boss $20,000 and my boss wants it. Seeing how your dad flew the coop, you're all the leverage we have. Unfortunately you're collateral damage." Trent explained.

I grimaced at that and blew hard out of my nose. I just nodded and looked out the window. I had nothing to say. What was there to say? My dad had royally screwed me over and he didn't care. He wouldn't care that these guys had me or what they did to me as long as he was safe. I could feel Trent watching me. I'm sure he thought I would have something to say, but I didn't want to say anything to him or anyone else for that matter. I just wanted Sal and unfortunately, I may be reunited with him soon and still a virgin. He should be proud. I wanted to cry, but I would not cry in front of this SOB.

I kept looking out the windows. I didn't know which way we had gone or where he was taking me until I saw the lights of Vegas come into view. Of course, Vegas, a gamblers favorite dream or worst nightmare. I wasn't a gambler and this was a nightmare. I felt Trent looking at me again. I let my head fall forward on my shoulders and I looked down at my feet. I said a silent prayer that they would just kill me and not force me into prostitution to pay back my father's debts. Then, I took a deep breath and straightened my shoulders and looked straight at Trent, "I hope we are almost to where we are going. I really need to pee."

He shook his head. "We are almost there. Dee I…uh…."

"Just don't say anything Trent. You've said and done enough. This all makes sense now." I said.

He looked at me again. "What makes sense?" He asked.

"You called me the night I graduated didn't you? It was you looking for my dad. You know I really have nothing to do with him, but I guess money talks more than my life. I kept feeling like someone was watching me and I even looked around. You were good. I never saw you. Then, stopping in at the shop. Boy you had me fooled. You even got a cherry coke. You must've really been watching me. Paying for an oil change and damn it all… I liked you. Goes to show I'm a bad judge of character and not near safe enough. After all the shit my father has done and me even paying off his debt at the age of 13, I'm going out now. Of course, right before I can get the hell out. But I guess I would never be safe with my sperm donor out there. Sooner or later someone would have gotten to me to try to get him to pay up. Do you seriously think, he's going to care you have me? I'll answer for you, no. He's never cared about me. I've been taking care of myself since I was ten!" The words came out of me in a torrent. I was angry and hurt and felt stupid.

I saw Trent flinch at my words. He then answered me, "I was watching you. I really never meant to find you. I was mesmerized by a chick who loved cars and yes, I wanted to see if you really knew what you were doing. You do. I did call looking for your father and was sure surprised to have a chick answer the phone. And while I'm being honest, I always get cherry coke. That wasn't for you. I was actually surprised we have the same drink of choice. You've been on your own since ten?"

I just nodded.

He finished for me, "Until Sal took you under his wing. He was a good man. I'm sorry you lost him."

"That's rich. You're sorry? Trent you kidnapped me. You can hardly be sorry for me losing Sal." I hissed at him.

"Look Dee, I know you loved Sal like a father. My father isn't the best man in the world but he loves me and was quick to tell me he was proud of me. I would be completely broken if I lost him. Just take a little kindness from me in your dark place." Trent said.

I was incredulous. "Seriously Trent? Take a little kindness from you. You are freaking making my place darker. I'm condemned for my father's sins. Life is just freaking fantastic. I don't want your kindness. Hell I don't want anything you have. Just kill me and get this over with and until then shut the hell up!"

He silently nodded.

Trent pulled down a back alley and went into a private parking garage. He parked Fiona and walked around and opened my door and grabbed me by the arm to let me out. I stood up right in front of him. He smelled so good and his five o'clock shadow was very becoming. Damn it head. Shut up. This guy kidnapped you. You can't think anything nice about him. He studied me a moment and I just stared right back. He pulled me forward and shut the door. I turned around and placed my tied hands on top of Fiona and whispered, "Bye girl."

Trent stiffened at that. I was resigned to my fate. There was nothing I could do at this point. I let him lead me to an elevator. I let my head rest against the wall. It was still pounding. I closed my eyes and saw Sal smile at me. I let my mouth soften and the corners turn up the slightest bit. Trent noticed. "What are you so content for?" He asked.

"I've learned to be content with little to nothing my whole life. This isn't any different and what I was thinking about is mine. It's not for you." I said with pain now in my eyes.

He just nodded and looked away. But I would lock eyes with him from time to time in the reflections on the shiny elevator doors. He really didn't seem like the goon type. I had come across those. But I guess that's why he was so good at his job.

The elevator dinged and the doors slid open. We were in a fancy penthouse. I had never seen anything like it before in my life. If I wasn't tied up, I would have loved being here. Trent led me to a bathroom. I held my hands up to him as if to ask, "How am I supposed to go with no hands?" He smiled at me and followed me in.

"What are you doing?" I asked frantically.

"You need to go to the bathroom and I can't untie you seeing how you attacked me earlier. I've got several knots on my head to prove it. It's not like anyone hasn't seen you naked before." He said.

I just stared at him dumbfounded.

He looked at me. Shock beginning to register on his face. "No one has seen you naked?"

I shook my head. I don't why I did. The last thing he needed to know was that. That's almost like telling him, "Oh by the way I'm a virgin, so if killing me isn't enough you could rape me first." I swallowed hard.

He swallowed hard. "Ok so, I'll look the other way. Promise."

"And how am I supposed to wipe? I don't like feeling unclean. I'm not going to air dry with your face turned away from me." I stated feeling the lump in my throat get bigger.

Trent looked at me. "I'll clean you."

"NO!!" I screamed. "I promise I won't try to come after you again or do anything foolish. Please just let me pee and wipe myself. When I give my word I mean it." I promised.

He searched my eyes and nodded. "I believe you. But I will have tie you back up before the boss gets here." He said.

He untied my hands and I immediately rubbed my wrists. Trent almost looked sad seeing me do that. I looked at him and he took the hint. He turned around. I went to the toilet and my hands trembled as I unbuttoned my pants and then unzipped them. The zipper seemed so loud in the bathroom and I could have sworn Trent tensed when he heard it too. I pulled my pants down and relieved myself. It was super awkward. I wiped and pulled my pants back up, flushed, and went to the sink. When I turned the faucet on, Trent turned around and looked at me. I splashed water on my face and then toweled off. I gave him back my hands and looked him in the eyes as he tied me back up. I didn't let my shoulders slump, though I wanted to. He led me out to a massive kitchen. It was very modern and the six burner stove was amazing. He pulled a chair from the table in an adjoining dining area and put it in the middle of the kitchen and sat me down, and retied my hands to the back of the chair facing him and the windows outside.

I looked past him to the city scape of Las Vegas. I could have appreciated that view under different circumstances. I felt numb. Too much had happened in one day. I finished Fiona, I lost Sal, I was kidnapped by a hot guy, I went to the bathroom with said guy in the room, and I allowed him to tie me back up, and now I sit helpless in a chair. I felt a pang in my gut. I had let Sal down. He had dreams for me too. We had just had such a deep conversation and he said he would like to be a Papa Sal. I hadn't thought much of having children. Now with the doom of my murder lingering over me, I thought I might really like to be a mom.

I looked back to Trent. He was studying me.  I just stared blankly at him. I didn't want him to read my emotions. He didn't deserve to see them, but oddly I felt pretty calm. Until, there was a ding and the elevator doors slid open. I couldn't see who it was, but I could hear the heavy footsteps coming up from a side hall. It must be the boss. I guess this must be his fancy place too. When he came into view, he looked like a straight up mob boss. He even had on a pin stripe suit! His salt and pepper hair was slicked back on his large head and he had deep set green eyes. He had olive colored skin and deep crow's feet. He also had wide shoulders and big hands that sported a wedding band and pinky rings.

His deep, Italian accented voice hit me. "Dee darlin. I'm sorry to have to meet you under such unpleasant circumstances. My name is Giorgio Moe Trentolini I didn't even know Brian had a daughter. How old are you?"

I held his gaze and decided to play along. I mean I was tied up. What else do you do besides answer the mob boss? "Well, you wouldn't know about me. My father doesn't give a rat's ass that he has a daughter. The man I considered my dad died earlier this evening. I'm eighteen." I answered.

His eyebrows shot up. "Oh only eighteen. You have only just begun. Your father should have taken better care. It seems so unfair that his troubles fall on you." Giorgio said.

"I would have to agree, but my father won't come for me. He's a selfish man. He's been leaving me to fend for myself since I was ten years old. I even paid one of his debts at just thirteen when I made it home to find a big, scary guy waiting on my dad. My life is just a never ending shit cycle from my father's decisions. Look, don't torture me. He won't care. He won't come and it won't make him get your money any faster. Just be a man and kill me and get it over with so we can all move on." I said on a long breath.

Giorgio studied me. He said, "I like your grit kid. Your dad is a pitiful excuse for a human. I really don't wish to hurt you. Hurting girls isn't my style. I'm a family man."

I started to laugh hysterically. Both men stared at me. "I'm sorry. You saying you're a family man when you had your goon follow me and kidnap me is just hilarious. You know you could of just asked me for help and told me the truth from the beginning. At this point I'd believe anything, but to kidnap me hardly makes me want to play nice or believe that you're a family man." I said still shaking with laughter.

Trent looked at me scornfully. I couldn't help it. When death should have me terrified, I felt brazen. Trent spoke up, "You really shouldn't speak that way of a man you don't know. It's not very nice."

I laughed even harder. "You want to talk about nice. You knocked me over the head, tied me up, and brought me here. You're a great judge of nice. You shouldn't kidnap someone you don't know." I said making an annoyed face at him.

Giorgio smirked. "You're right she's a wild one son. I like her."

My head spun. "What? Son?" I asked confused.

Giorgio spoke again, "Yes Dee darlin. My goon, Trent, is short for Trentolini. His mother calls him Giorgie of course."

"You should have at casino drink named after you. The Trentolini would be a good play on a martini." I said for no reason. Both men were looking at me again. "I'm just saying. It makes sense." I added.

Then they laughed.

"Oh what to do with you Dee. Maybe send a picture to you father. Or you do have that nice car I could sale for what he owes me." Giorgio thought out loud.

I screamed, "No. Don't touch Fiona. She's all I have."

Both men jumped and looked at me.

"Let me talk to my son. As far as I'm concerned you can be his to deal with. I'll give him my advice of course." Giorgio said with a glint in his eyes.

I smiled overly exaggerated and said, "Of course."

Chapter 8

Both men had walked off somewhere to talk about what to do with me. Sal would want me to fight for my life, but I was too tired to care. I heard the elevator doors close and heard the footsteps headed back towards me. I caught his eyes when he got in view.

I looked into the gorgeous green eyes staring at me. This man was tall with dark hair fashionably cut and a hard jawline with a sexy five o'clock shadow. He was staring down at me as I sat tied to a chair in the middle of a penthouse kitchen. "At least he's hot," was all I could think. I wasn't scared like I should be. I didn't imagine I would die like this, but if I had to go at least I had some eye candy to look at. Deep down, I guess I had to know this was a possibility. Funny thing is, I wasn't sure how to feel. To know that you're the only good thing your father ever did in his life, felt big and oddly reassuring in my last moment. I wondered if my death would finally make my dad grow the hell up and be a decent person.

The man slowly started to stalk towards me. I locked my brown eyes with his green ones. I wanted him to see me and know that I would meet my death with my pride intact. I wanted him to see that I was nothing like the man who had a hand in making me. I was not a coward and if I had to pay the price for his lifestyle, I'd do it my way. The man slowed and stopped to stare. I wasn't begging for my life and I wouldn't. No one would mourn me, except maybe my dad and that was a hard maybe.

He started to come towards me again. I could see the knife in his hand. I wouldn't let him know that the sight of that did make me flinch on the inside. Death didn't scare me, but I wasn't a friend to pain. I hoped he did it quickly. I still uttered not a word. I kept my eyes locked with his and for some unknown reason, I smiled. I freaking smiled at him. He raised his hand with the knife, I stared, and he bent to be only inches from my face. I could feel his breath on me. His nose was almost touching mine. My breath stilled and for the first time I was really nervous. He reached his hand behind me with the knife and cut my bindings.

I didn't move to get up. I was paralyzed and our eyes were locked still with his face so close to mine. My breast were heaving up with the extra effort to just breathe. He looked down at them and quirked a smile. I got mad and I turned red.

"Are you just playing with me? I don't want to play cat and mouse. Whatever you're going to do, do it fast." I demanded.

He tilted his head sideways and looked at me hard. He was still holding the knife. I was very aware of that. I kept my shoulders tall. I wouldn't show weakness to him. He was still looking at me and I saw his eyes search my face and land on my lips. In an instant he closed the small space and pressed his lips to mine hard.

I tried to back my head away, but there was nowhere for me to go. The knife was still in his hand and I was still in a chair. He kissed more insistently. I was rigid and nervous. He stuck his tongue out to tease my lips. He wanted me to kiss him back. I didn't want to. I sat still.

Trent pulled away. "I'm sorry. I just…I wanted to….I couldn't help it." He stuttered out.

I was livid. "You couldn't help it? That's funny. I don't know why you would think I would want you to kiss me after you kidnapped me today. That's freaking crazy. I hope you kill me soon. To think I got my first kiss at knife point and I didn't participate or enjoy it. This day or night or whatever it is just keeps getting better and better."

Trent stood up quickly and threw the knife. He looked terrible. He stared down at me and almost looked sorry. He said, "Dee. I didn't mean to. I forgot I even had the knife and I wasn't trying to force you to kiss me. I mean, I wanted to kiss you. Damn. I didn't know…If I'd known you'd never been kissed…I'd…"

I cut him off, "You'd what? Put rose petals down? Take me dinner? Kiss me on top of a Ferris wheel? You don't even know a thing about me Trent and to just assume I would want that. You must be pretty smart to find me and follow me without me knowing, but what you just did was a dumb jerk move. You really forgot you had a knife?"

Trent moved and picked the knife up and went and put it away. He walked back to in front of me. "I was caught in the moment and now stepping back and looking at it, I can see how it would be a terrible moment for you and I'm sorry. I mean that. I'm not going to kill you. I couldn't. I've been mesmerized by you since I first heard you on the phone. I do have to try to get the money out of your father though, somehow."

"You held me a gun point earlier and you say you couldn't kill me? Forgive me for finding all this hard to believe." I spat out.

"Dee the gun wasn't loaded. I was hoping you would just do what I asked, but no you had to come at me with a screwdriver and I have the lumps to show for that. But, I guess thinking about it, you really didn't want to kill me either or you would have stabbed me instead of hitting me with the handle." He said smiling at me again.

"I'm not a murderer." I said finally looking away. He caught my weakness.

"And you said you liked me and I have gorgeous eyes." He prodded.

"That was before all this," I said throwing my hands around. I finally let my head fall into my hands and rubbed my temples.

"You're tired and had a long day. Let me get you some water and aspirin. How about a nice shower or bath? I have a big jacuzzi tub you're welcome to use." Trent said moving to a cabinet to pull a glass down and go to the refrigerator and get me some water from the door.

I stared in disbelief. What the heck was happening? "You're worried about my head and you want me to take a shower? If you're not going to kill me then why can't I just leave?" I asked.

"I know by the way things have happened you can't tell, but I like you Dee. I really am sorry about Sal and I never wanted to hurt you. Let me take care of you for tonight. I can't let you leave until I decide what to do about the money and your dad." He informed me.

I nodded. So I'm not going to die tonight at least. I replied, "I don't have any clothes here and I'm not walking around naked."

He chuckled. "I have a robe you can use and I'll buy you some clothes tomorrow." He handed me the water and the aspirin.

I took it, because honestly my head hurt really bad. I asked, "You're not going to sit in the bathroom while I bathe are you?"

"Only if you want me to," said Trent wiggling his eyebrows.

"Yeah, that's a hard no. Go grab me that robe. I still smell like paint fumes." I said breathing out deeply.

Trent looked at me a long moment and said, "Ok. I promise not to hurt you again or do anything without talking to you about it first. I'll even take you to see Vegas tomorrow if you want."

I nodded and just said, "That robe will be nice for now, but Trent I have to go back home. Sal..His funeral needs to be planned. I'm all he has."

I tried to hide my tears, but they filled my eyes and Trent was back in front of me on his knees. He grabbed my knees with his hands and squeezed. "Will you let me hug you?" He asked.

I nodded in a moment of weakness and fell into his arms and he held me tight. I literally cried on his shoulder. For the first time I could remember, I lost it and needed to be held. I had cried with Sally in the parking lot, but this was different. I was crying for more than just losing Sal and I was feeling way too much. Wanting to be touched was foreign to me. I lost my dad and my real dad got me into this mess and this hot guy kidnapped me and now offered to take care of me. My mind was a swirling mess. He was rubbing my back and saying soothing things, when I straightened up and wiped my eyes. I looked at him and nodded.

 "Come on. I'll take you to my master bath. That's where the big tub is." He said reaching down and grabbing my hand.

"So this is your place?" I asked.

He just nodded and led me through a giant bedroom to a huge bathroom. He got me towel out of a cabinet and grabbed me a washcloth. Then, he marched out to his closet and grabbed a black robe and set it on the back of the toilet for me.

"If you need anything, just holler. I'll make us a bite to eat." He said and then disappeared.

I was in shock. What the hell was going on? I looked around the big bathroom. It was a light blue with white trim and pictures of the ocean hung on the wall behind the toilet. The bathtub was magnificent. I went to start the water and get it just right. I took my clothes off as it was filling up. My head was still hurting. I sank into the tub and started the jets. I let out a sigh. I needed this. I wet the wash cloth and set it over my face and tried to make sense of all that was going on. There was no sense to be made. I was essentially a prisoner. In a really nice prison, but prisoner.

Chapter 9

"Dee! Dee! Wake up Dee! Please be ok!" I could hear the screaming, but I couldn't will me eyes to open. Was I dreaming? I felt like I was floating and I was so warm. Yes dreaming. I was relaxed.

"Damn it Dee! I did this to you. God I'm sorry. Please open your eyes!" A frantic man yelled.

I knew that voice. It was Trent. I felt my blood run cold. Where was I? Oh yes a prisoner. But why is he so worried about waking me up? What's the big deal? OH. MY. GOD. He left me to take a bath. I felt my pulse quicken. I could still feel the water around me like a warm blanket. I'm still in the tub. I'm still naked. Trent is in here and I'm naked. If I wasn't close to dying, I would die now.

"Dee baby. Please open your eyes. You've got to be ok." Trent whispered as he ran his hands down my face to my neck. He was checking for my pulse. I'm pretty sure my heart was going to beat out my chest. He ran his hands back to my head and was rubbing. Then, fireworks shot through me as he touched a very painful knot at the base of my skull. That's where he had hit me with the gun. My eyes clinched tighter from the pain and I let out a moan.

"Dee can you hear me?" Trent asked sounding shaky. "Dee?"

I tried to answer, but all I could do was moan again.

"I'm going to get you out of this tub and call a doctor. I know I promised I wouldn't touch you again without asking, but you're giving me no choice. I have to get you help." Trent said quickly.

My mind was reeling. I'm giving him no choice? He didn't give me a choice when he kidnapped me!

I felt a strong arm go under my bottom and then settle behind my knees and I felt his other arm slide around me under my armpits and settle at my ribcage. He was going to try to lift me out of a tub soaking wet and as dead wet. Yeah good luck with that buddy. But, then I was gliding out of the water and cradled to his strong body and moving somewhere. He laid me down on a bed and used his hand to push the hair off my face. I moaned again and he stopped abruptly.

I heard him walk off somewhere and then I heard him on the phone as he came back to me. "Doc. It's Trent. I need you at my penthouse now. My guest has a lump on her head and I found her unconscious in the bathtub. Her heartrate seems ok and she's breathing, but I can't get her to wake up. She's moaning some. Please hurry. I'll pay you for your time and then some."

Then, I felt him beside me and he was towel drying me. He was so gentle. He rubbed my feet and massaged my hands and rubbed down my whole body. I should be so angry, but it felt good. It felt comforting. But, I was naked. He was seeing me completely naked. Next, I felt him pulling the covers over my nakedness.

"Dee. I'm so damn sorry Dee. I never wanted to hurt you. I had to defend myself when you came at me with that damn screwdriver. I know you don't want to admit it, but you didn't want to hurt me either. Shit, I've got to be crazy to think you could ever look at me with anything other than disdain. I want you Dee baby and I want you to want me. I can't help it. It wasn't part of the job to want to get to know you. I want to know everything about you. You've got to be one of toughest people I know. Would you believe me if I told you I actually told my Pop about all this earlier? I told him I wouldn't let anything else bad happen to you, because you have already been through enough in your short lifetime and I would figure out how to get his money back without any harm coming to you. I..I feel connected to you somehow. Please Dee baby, be ok." I felt the last part whispered on my forehead as he pressed his lips into my head.

The elevator dinged. Trent got up quickly and headed towards the elevator. "Thanks for coming so quickly Doc. She's in here on my bed." Trent said.

"What's her name?" Doc asked.

"Dee. Her name is Dee. She's eighteen and she got knocked on the back of the head earlier tonight and she suffered the loss of her dad on top of all that." Trent filled him in.

All I could think was, "Sal. My dad. I want to see you again, but I'm not sure I'm ready yet."

I felt cold hands at the base of my skull and then I felt a cold, round, metal object at my chest. Oh he's listening to my heart I realized. Why can't I open my eyes? Why can't I speak? I was getting scared. I moaned again as he touched the lump on my head. Trent quickly came over and grabbed my hand. His hand was warm and engulfed mine.

"Dee baby. I'm right her. Doc is here to help you. You will be ok," said Trent squeezing my hand.

Doc spoke then, "I'm going to give her an IV. She's very dehydrated. She's suffered a lot of trauma and from the amount of crying I'm sure she's done, she's low on fluids. First we have to hydrate her. Second, she has a concussion. Luckily, the swelling is mostly out so that's good, but it is most likely pushing on the part of the brain that allows her to open her eyes. We have to get the swelling down. Third, the poor girl is probably just over exhausted from everything that's happened."

"She's going to be ok though?" Trent asked

"Yes she should be fine as soon as the swelling goes down and we get some fluids in her," said Doc.

"Thank God. Thank you Doc. I couldn't bare for her to not be ok." Trent said finally sounding a little less stressed.

"I'll take good care of her. I need to start her IV now. I'll give her fluids and medication to help the swelling. She should be fine in the morning. I'll came back at nine to take her IV out if she's doing well, but you'll need to stay close to her incase anything changes." Doc explained.

"I will. What do you need me to do now Doc?" asked Trent.

"Just sit by her and let me fix her up." Doc said.

I think I could hear a smile in his voice. Apparently he was moved by Trent's concern for me. I didn't understand why he was so concerned over me. I had heard his kind words earlier, but there was no way he could actually care about me. He didn't even know me and I didn't know him at all. I wasn't going there. Not now.

I felt the prick of the needle in my arm as he did the IV. I didn't moan until I felt the cool liquid going into my veins. "Is she ok?" Trent asked.

"She's fine. She can still feel everything and probably hear everything too. The swelling is just suppressing certain functions for the time being," said Doc.

I felt Doc put something cool on my bump and then a heart rate monitor on my finger. "If anything at all changes, call me right away. I'll have my phone on me all night." Doc said as he rubbed my arm.

"I will. Thank you so much Doc. So you think she can hear me?" Trent asked.

"That's a very likely possibility. Call me if you need to. Other than that I'll see you at nine." Doc said and he walked out and left.

I heard Trent let out a deep breath and he leaned down to head and kissed my forehead and said, "I'm sorry Dee."

Then, I heard him shuffle away to the bathroom and I heard the water run. When he came out, I heard him unzip his pants. My insides screamed. I moaned. I wanted to say don't. Please don't do that to me too. I can't even open my eyes. I next, heard him go to his closet and a drawer closing. What is he doing? I wondered.

I felt the bed dip as he crawled in next to me. I wanted to cry. I had already lost Sal and been kidnapped. I couldn't handle being raped too. I just couldn't. I wanted my first time to be special and full of love. I wanted it to be nothing like the first kiss I had unwillingly gotten tonight. I was surprised when Trent didn't do anything. He just grabbed my hand, laced our fingers together, and set my hand down over his heart. I could feel his heart beating and I could feel the smoothness of his chest. He didn't have a shirt on.

"Dee, I don't know if you can really hear me or not, but Doc said maybe. At least you can't argue with me or tell me how wrong I am at every turn. You have no choice but to listen, so I'm going to talk." Trent said as he squeezed my hand.

He went on, "I ended up coming to your small town looking for Brian. My dad isn't a bookie creep. He's a loan shark, but mostly a good one. He tries to help out guys who get in with the bad ones. He even sets up reasonable payment plans or even will let the guys work off the debts in his casino or hotel. He's not always a good guy. When there's so much money involved things can get a little crazy. Brian has owed my Pop that money for over five years. He tried to help him, but Brian is always a flake. Oh and hey it was really funny earlier when you told Pop he should have a martini named after him. You had no way to know he owned a casino, but that was golden. I bet he does have a drink named after him the next time I go or maybe we go to the casino."

He paused thinking. "Or maybe that's a terrible idea. You probably don't want to step foot in a casino after all your father, I mean Brian, has done. I won't call him your father. He doesn't deserve that title. I saw earlier when Sal crumpled and you held him in your arms. You are so strong Dee baby. The truth is, I've done nothing but watch you since the day after your graduation. I know you don't know me, but I know you. I know your habits, what makes you smile, what you love, and what upsets you. I was completely captivated by such a beautiful, fast car loving, mechanic, who chose happiness, even though her situation wasn't ideal. I watched you close your eyes and take in the warmth of the sun as you rode your bike and I wished I could give you that peace." He squeezed my hand again.

"But all I've brought you is more pain and all I want you to do is flash your beautiful smile at me like you did when we talked in the shop. I want to share a real cherry coke with you and I want to watch you suck on your cherry tootsie pop. I want to kiss you while your mouth still tastes of cherry. I bet you taste good mixed with the cherry of the sucker. I'm sorry if that freaks you out, but I'm laying my heart out here. I'm not sure if I really want you to hear all of this or not. I had no idea you'd never been kissed. I would like a do-over on that one. I just can't imagine a beautiful, driven woman like you never being kissed. I can only imagine what else you haven't done and selfishly I'm glad. The thought of someone else touching you, makes my blood boil. Dee baby I know you deserve so much better than me. I don't even know if this thing is something that could work, but I would regret it for my entire life if I didn't try. I want to be the reason that you smile. I want to buy tons of classic cars for you to fix. I want to take you to dinner and let everyone stare at the beautiful woman on my arm. Dee I want to give you the life you deserve."

He finished up then with, "I know I've screwed all that up. I freaked out and didn't know what to do. I just knew I had to get you to come with me and I knew my Pop had to see I followed through. I'm actually a private investigator and help my father run the hotel. I'm honestly not much on the casino believe it or not. Now, I'm going to shut up. I don't know if you heard a word I said, but I'm not going to leave your side and I'll stay here all night holding your hand. Dee I um..Dee."

Chapter 10

I finally opened my eyes at seven thirty in the morning. The sun was peeking in through the bedroom windows. It hurt my head at first, but then everything came clear into view. The room was immaculate. It had grey walls with white trim and the bedroom furniture was black and he had paintings of the black night sky with the moon in every phase on the walls. The sheer curtains were also black. I realized I was in a king size, four post bed, with beautiful wood carvings. I looked to my left and saw Trent, laying on his back, my hand still held in his to his chest. The sun was hitting his face and he was beautiful. I wanted to touch his jaw and run my fingers across his more than a five o' clock shadow now, but I didn't. I couldn't allow myself to feel anything but anger. He followed me and kept me in the dark. Things could have been so much different if he would have just told me from the beginning.

I had heard everything he said though. He didn't do anything, but hold my hand and he had poured his heart out to me. There's no way he could actually have real feelings for me in such a short time. He couldn't possibly really feel all that. I believed he did feel bad and he had taken care of me all night, but seriously? This was a lot to take in. I studied his face. Why did he have to be so hot?

I don't know if I moved or he could feel me staring at him, but his eyes shot open. I didn't say a word, I just kept looking at him. His eyes searched my face. I looked down at my hand in his on his chest and he followed my gaze. He let go and brought his hand to the side of my face. "You're ok?" He breathed out.

I just nodded.

"Could you hear me last night?" He asked.

I nodded again, never taking my eyes off of his. His eyes searched mine. I wasn't sure what for, but I wasn't ready for that conversation yet. I just woke up after not being able to open my eyes or talk.

"I need to go to the bathroom." I croaked out.

He nodded and smiled. He got out of bed and came around to help me up and I noticed he was only in navy blue briefs and seemed, let's just say, happy. I quickly looked away. I blushed.

Trent laughed, "It's ok. It won't bite you. I need to go to the bathroom too. It's first thing in the morning. This is pretty normal."

I felt him gently grab my arm and put his other behind my back to help me sit up. I groaned. I felt like I had been run over by a train. "You ok?" He asked quickly.

"Yes. I just feel so sore." I replied.

Trent got me to my feet and I stood for a moment to gain my composure and balance. Then, I looked down to notice, I was still naked. I looked up to Trent horrified. He noticed the look on my face and turned his head away.

"It's ok Dee. You're beautiful and I saw all of you last night when I had to scoop you out of the water. Thank God, I came to check on you when you'd been in for so long. You could have slid down and..I just can't think about that. Please don't feel embarrassed or ashamed around me. It's ok. The robe I grabbed for you last night is still in the bathroom. You can put it on when you get in there. " Trent said.

"Ok." I breathed out quietly and he looked back to me.

He looked straight into my eyes and said, "Ok."

He moved around me to my other side and hooked his arm around my back and grabbed the IV pole to take it with me to the bathroom. When we got in there, he situated the IV pole by the toilet. "Are you ok if I leave so you can go by yourself?"

I nodded to him and he swiftly walked out. I immediately sat on the toilet. I felt so much better after going. Then I heard a knock at the door a few minutes later. "You ok Dee?" He asked.

"Actually," I said, "I need some help."

He gently opened the door to see me still standing naked in his bathroom, holding his robe. He took in a sharp breath. I noticed he wasn't as happy now. He must've gone to the other bathroom.

"What do you need Dee?" He asked.

I held the robe up and said, "I can't get it on by myself with this IV. I'm scared I'll rip it out."

Trent instantly moved to me and grabbed the robe. He held it open and helped me get my free arm in first and then gently got the other arm in with the IV and then rolled the sleeve up so it wouldn't be pulling on my IV. Next, he stepped behind me, his body touching mine, and wrapped his arms around me with his chin on my shoulder and closed the robe up and tied it shut. I was trembling.

"You're trembling Dee. Do you need to sit? Are you ok?" He rapidly asked.

"I uh..I'm ok. I just..You've seen me naked and I've never....I've never been that close to anyone before. I guess I'm a freak." I said looking down.

"No one has ever held you intimately at all? You're no freak Dee. You're perfect." He said still holding onto me tight from behind, his chin still resting on my shoulder.

"I bet I'm not so perfect." I said starting to laugh.

Trent raised an eyebrow.

"I have alligator breath. I really need to brush my teeth," I said laughing some, almost forgetting I was a prisoner. Almost.

Trent let out a little laugh to. "Well, you're in luck. It just so happens I buy my toothbrushes in a two pack. I have an extra." He left me to go to the sink and got in the second drawer under it and pulled out a purple toothbrush and handed it to me.

I gingerly walked to the sink. He scooted over and put a glob of toothpaste on my toothbrush and then put some on his and turned the water on. I just looked at him. This was all so weird.

"You just going to stare at me or brush your teeth?" He asked around the toothbrush in his mouth.

I chuckled and shook my head and started to brush my teeth next to the navy blue brief, shirtless Trent. This was all surreal. I went from doing everything by myself to brushing my teeth with Trent. It was a lot to take in. I spit and swirled water around in my mouth and then checked my teeth in the mirror. Trent was smiling as he watched me.

"What?" I asked.

"Nothing. I just love everything you do. Who would've of thought I would like watching someone brush their teeth?" He said shaking his head and walking off.

"Where are you going?" I asked.

"To make us some coffee and breakfast. We didn't eat dinner last night." He said walking out of his room towards the kitchen.

I followed slowly behind him, carefully to roll my IV with me. I was trying to hold onto my anger. It was hard to when I really took in all that was Trent. He was standing by his coffee pot filling it with water when I walked in. His back was to me. He was in amazing shape. He had a nice hard butt, a muscled back, and his legs were all muscle. He was also a nice tan color. He turned around to see me studying him. The front was even better than the back. He had the sexy v thing going on and you could wash clothes on those abs. He didn't have a hairy chest, but it was broad and his face. Oh his face was like a Calvin Klein model. His emerald green eyes pierced through me. I never wanted to admit it, but the day he was in the shop is when I decided to paint Fiona green.

"What's running through that pretty head of yours?" He asked as he returned my gaze.

I felt my face go hot. I prayed he couldn't tell what I was thinking. "I don't think you want to know." I said.

"Judging by that blush on your cheeks, I think I do," said Trent smiling like the devil he was.

"I'm f'ing pissed Trent. I heard all the things you said last night and to be honest, they seem unbelievable. Why wouldn't you just tell me the truth? This situation could be so much different had you just been honest. I'm mad that I pee'd in front of you. I'm mad that I like your bathtub. I'm mad that you saw me naked. I'm mad that I'm so vulnerable in front of you. I'm mad that you are so sweet. I'm mad that you have to be gorgeous in every way possible. I'm made the most intimate moments of my life are tainted with being held prisoner. I'm mad that I don't want to mad at you right now! I should be running for the hills and yet I want to be here with you. What in the actual hell is wrong with me?" I screamed.

Trent tensed. I just threw a lot at him and he deserved every bit of it. Trent stalked over to me and I tensed then. He put his hands on my face and asked, "You're mad you like my bathtub?"

I started laughing and he laughed. Then he stopped and looked into my eyes. "You have every right to be mad. You are not my prisoner. I want you to want to be here with me, because God Dee, I want you here. I'm sorry I royally f'ed everything up. I'm a stupid man. I'm vulnerable with you too Dee. I poured my heart out to you. I didn't mean to ruin your most intimate moments. I don't want to do that. But you think I'm gorgeous in every way possible?" He asked wiggling his eyebrows.

"Giorgie boy  I think you know that your gorgeous." I said poking fun at him.

"Oh no. You can't call me Giorgie! That's a total buzz kill. Knowing that you think I'm gorgeous though…That's something special. Do I have a chance to fix this Dee?" He asked.

I looked at him. I wasn't sure what to say. I wasn't sure if he was worthy of me and all Sal wanted was for me to find someone worthy of me. I answered honestly, "I don't know. I don't know how to be with someone and I'm not sure that I can get over you pointing a gun at me and keeping me here. Trent, I need to go home. I have to lay Sal to rest. After all he's done for me, I have to at least to that."

Trent nodded at me and said, "Then, I'll go back with you. You don't have to do it alone. Can I hug you Dee? I feel like I need to wrap my arms around you."

I slowly nodded and he wrapped his arms around me, one at my waist and one around my shoulder and he held me tight. I closed my eyes and allowed myself to let him hold me up if only for a moment. He kissed the top of my head and I pulled away. He looked at me and his face was soft.

"Go sit down at the bar. I'll cook for you," said Trent.

I did as I was told. He poured me a cup of coffee and put two scoops of sugar and splash of half and half, just the way I liked it. I eyed him. "I paid real close attention to you Dee." He said.

"I know nothing about you Trent. Spill it," I said.

He quirked a smile at me and said, "Ok."

He turned away and started to crack eggs into a bowl and said, "My name is Giorgio Moe Trentolini Jr. I like my coffee black. My favorite food is my Ma's lasagna. My birthday is June 2. I'm twenty six years old. I graduated at the top of my class. I went to the police academy and could be a cop, but I make more money as a PI. I help my Pop with the running of the hotel. I want to get married and have kids one day. I was born entitled. My grandfather owned the casino that my Pop now owns and my Pop purchased the hotel a few years back. I have never been hungry or worried about bills. My father, though a hard ass, is a great father. He always showed me and my sister love. He treats my Ma like the queen she is. My sister is two years younger than me and she runs the boutique in the casino. Her name is Lillian. She is my best friend. She is married and I have a little niece, Haley, I adore. I love fast cars, but I think you know that. I'm terrified of being a failure and I'm terrified of how strongly I feel for you and I hate myself for hurting you. I did that to you and you could of died last night. I don't deserve any part of you, but I'm hoping you can see through my shit and just maybe find something you like besides my gorgeous face."

I stared dumbfounded. He was bold if nothing else. We were like the Lady and the Tramp, but me being the tramp. We were from two different sides of the track and that scared me and it scared me how open he was with wanting me for more than a friend. I was having a hard time processing it all.

"Trent, I don't know about all this. You have no idea the life I've lived. You just think I'm interesting. I don't trust you. You make me nervous." I replied.

He looked at me with sorrow in his eyes and said, "I know you don't trust me, but I promise to earn it if you let me. How about we try to be friends? Can we do that?"

I looked at him for a long time and said, "Friends."

He nodded and got back to making us breakfast and I heard the elevator ding.

"Giorgie it's me." A woman's voice called and I immediately stiffened.

Was his booty call really showing up while I'm sitting right here?

"In the kitchen Sis." He called back.

I felt stupid. Why was I getting mad if there was a woman in his life?

His sister, Lilian, turned into the kitchen and gasped. "Oh sweetheart. Are you ok?" She asked heading straight for me.

My eyes went wide. "I'm fine. I'm Dee. You must be Lilian." I said.

"Nice to meet you Dee. Giorgie told me he needed clothes for a woman that stayed with him. I was shocked to get the call. I didn't imagine I would find said woman in his robe with and IV hooked to her arm." She hissed towards her brother.

Trent grimaced. Clearly he left some parts out. "Thank you for bringing her some clothes Sis. You hungry? I'm making us some breakfast and the coffee is hot." He offered.

His sister studied him. "What the hell is going on Giorgie? Did Daddy put you up to something crazy? And why does this beautiful flower have an IV in her arm?" Lilian asked with her hands on her hips.

I broke in to help him out. I don't know why, but I did. "I thought only your mom called you Giorgie. If she gets to call you Giorgie, then I do too." I smiled like the Cheshire cat at him.

He groaned and Lilian busted out laughing. "Oh you're a good one Dee. I like you! And you're already covering for him. You're in deep and you don't even know it my flower. You have to be wary of these Italian men." She said looking me over.

I liked that she called me her flower. I smiled at her. "I don't know if I would say I'm in deep, but I'm definitely in waters that aren't normal for me." I answered.

Trent watched our exchange from the stove where he was sautéing bell peppers, mushroom, and onions. His mouth was soft and the corners were slightly turned up.

Lilian broke back in, "Dee, why do you have an IV in your arm in my brother's penthouse instead of being in a hospital?"

I looked over to Trent and he looked at me. I answered, "I got a nasty knot on my head. I'm ok though. Working in a mechanic shop can be risky business sometimes." I finished.

"You work in a mechanic shop. Well makes sense why my brother would be drooling over you. He has an unhealthy obsession with that orange car," said Lilian.

"Be quiet Sis. Tammy will hear you. She doesn't need to know she's my side chick now that Dee is here." He teased.

I turned red.

"Oh so she's your side chick now. Dee you must have a velvet…"

"Lilian! No. Don't go there." Trent bellowed after cutting her off abruptly.

I was confused. What was she talking about? I must have a velvet what? Then understanding dawned on me and I looked up wide eyed and I'm sure blushing big time. Both of them realized that I understood in that moment. Trent looked sorry. Lilian did not. She laughed.

"Oh girl. Just own it. If you got it, use it. No one has ever had any pull on my big brother. And plus you are naturally beautiful! We are going to be great friends." She said excitedly.

I was dumbstruck. I had no words.

"Giorgie, did you get a new car? I like that green one. She's sexy." Lilian said.

I had words now, "No. That's Fiona. She's mine. I just finished working on her and getting her makeup done. She is sexy. I'm glad you like her."

Lilian's smile got huge. "That's your car? And you fixed her? That's a bad ass girl ride!" She hollered.

Trent was smiling now at our exchange. He relaxed now.

"Yes. She's my dream car. I grew up in a mechanic shop. The guy that was basically my dad taught me everything I know and I mechanic'd in his shop with him. Sal. He was amazing. He bought her for me and she didn't run and needed a paint job so bad. I just finished her yesterday." Then, my face went sad, "And I also lost my dad, Sal, yesterday. Heart attack. The best day of my life, quickly turned into the worst."

Trent's shoulders slumped hearing my last words and I noticed them. My heartache really seemed to affect him. Lilian's face went soft and her eyes teared up and she pulled me into a tight hug. I looked up to see Trent's eyes on us. I slowly wrapped my arms around his sister and squeezed back.

"I'm so sorry Dee. I can't imagine. If I can do anything for you, you make sure and let me know. Do you have a phone? Let me put my number in it." She said.

I looked at Trent and said, "I don't know where my phone is. I seemed to have misplaced it."

Trent pulled his scrambled egg, vegetable skillet off the stove and filled three plates with food and walked out of the kitchen. He came back with my phone and handed it to his sister. "Here put your number in there for her. She could use a friend I'm sure. You know how it can be dealing with me."

She smiled and said, "That I do know. Dee you only have two phone numbers in here?"

"Sal just bought it for me yesterday. I hadn't had time to add anyone, not that I have anyone to really put in there. I'm more of a loner." I said.

"Well, now there are three numbers, your dad, Giorgie, and me. I mean it my flower. You call me if you need anything. I'm good at talking bad about my brother and I can listen. I'm also good for retail therapy. Speaking of which, Giorgie asked me to bring you some clothes. I brought a few things for you. I wasn't sure what you would like," she said.

"I don't know what to say. Thank you. I'll pay you for them as soon as I get my stuff together." I said quickly.

Trent broke in here, "No you won't. I owed you a shirt anyways remember?"

I smiled thinking back to when I got oil on my shirt working on Tammy. "But that's way more than a shirt. I can't possibly accept all of that." I said.

"Nonsense. You can and you will. My brother's girl will always have nice clothes. What good am I as sister that runs a boutique if you don't get to enjoy the clothes? Plus, Giorgie gets the family discount. You let him spoil you." Lilian said.

"This breakfast is really good. Thank you Trent and thank you for getting your sister to get me clothes," I said meaning it.

He smiled at me and said, "I'll give you the world if you let me."

I turned away and blushed.

Lilian gave out a squeal. "Am I finally going to get the sister I always wanted?"

She hugged me again. "Ok my flower, I have to get to work. I'll stop and get you real soon and we will go to lunch and have a girls' day. Feel better soon! I'll leave you two lovebirds to it. If you don't like any of the clothes, just let me know. Bye guys!" She said and jumped off her stool, kissed her brother on the cheek, and headed for the elevator.

I just sat on the stool quietly, wondering what the heck just happened. Lilian was amazingly sweet, she thought I was her brother's girl, that I had a velvet..Ya know, and that I was going to be her sister. This was crazy.

Chapter 11

After Lilian got in the elevator and she was for sure out of ear shot, Trent turned and looked at me. I was stirring the food around on my plate with my fork.

"If you don't like it, you don't have to it Dee." He said.

"Actually when I said breakfast was really good, I meant it. I love eggs and bell peppers. I'm just a little shocked at what just happened here." I said motioning to the clothes and the elevator.

"Yeah. Lilian can get a little out of control. It looks like she had fun shopping for you. She means well. And uh, thanks, for covering for me. You could have told her the truth about your IV and knot on your head. She would have literally taken the kitchen knife to me had she known." Trent said.

I looked at him a moment and then said, "I really like your sister. She is a sweet soul and really I just didn't want to upset her. She obviously loves her big brother. But, the velvet comment...that really shocked me. I..."

"That was out of line. I'm sorry. We are very open. My sister knows everything about me and for me to be so taken with you...She just assumed." Trent interrupted me.

I nodded. "And my phone?" I asked.

"I really never had any intention of keeping it from you. I picked up last night after our bad encounter. I noticed only Sal's number in there and assumed it would mean something to ya. I added my number, because you need it in case you need something if I'm at work or something." Trent explained.

"What exactly are your plans with me Trent. Am I held hostage or what? I'm so confused. You treat me like shit yesterday, then treat me like a guest, buy me clothes, tell me you'd give me the world, tell me I have to stay here until you get your money, and then say I need your number in case you're not here?" I asked not understanding at all what he was getting at.

"I don't want you to be my hostage. I want you to be my partner. Together we can come up with a solution with Brian and the money. I'm going to take you back to Sal's after Doc checks you out, so you can handle his funeral and I want to be there to help you. Then, we will come back here and figure the rest out," said Trent.

"Trent, I have plans for my life. I am supposed to be going to college this week. I'm supposed to making something of myself. I'm supposed to lose the stigma of my biological father and be better than him. I can't do all that living here and accepting handouts. I'm not a leech nor a beggar and I don't like to owe anyone anything." I said firmly.

"So go to college here. I don't like the idea of you having no one anymore Dee. I know you don't talk about it, but Sal was all you had. Let me be here for you. I'm not giving you a handout. I knocked you over the head. This is the least I can do. Honestly Dee, you can act like this house is yours. If you want to paint something, do it. I don't want to hold you back. You want your own mechanic shop? I'll be your business partner and help you get started. Let me be there for you. Please." Trent pleaded with me.

I looked up with a light in my eyes. "I have an idea. What if your Pop buys some old cars and I fix them up for him and he sells them and doubles his money? He could get his twenty grand and then some. Would I still have to worry about what Brian did? I hate the idea of working his debt off, but I do enjoy my cars."

"I think that's a great idea. I don't like the idea of you doing anything for your father's debt either, but my Pop is out the money. I could find you some sexy cars to work on too. I'll bring it up to Pop. We have a warehouse you could turn into a makeshift shop." Trent said getting excited.

"Ok. I can do this and be done with it all. I'll just do online courses for this first semester so I have time to work on the cars I need to get your Pop his money and I'll stay here in the meantime. We are just friends Trent." I said looking him in the eye.

"Sure. Just friends. Until you ask for something more," said Trent with a wicked smile on his face.

"I'm not going to Trent. Too much has happened already. I'll be honest with you, because I think you've been honest about your feelings with me. I'm an eighteen year old who has never even been on a date. I was always embarrassed of my home, my father, and my mother ran out on him when I was ten. I was never ready to try the relationship thing. My father has never hugged me, told me he loved me, or really just acknowledge I'm even around. I'm not sure how to do love, devotion, or intimacy. I'm a weirdo who has never been kissed or…ya know. It's a delicate thing for me. I want to love the person I choose that with. Before Sal died, he had told me no one would ever be good enough for me, but to find someone worthy of me. I'm not sure a guy who kidnaps me is worthy. I'm also uncomfortable as hell, because you've seen me naked and vulnerable and I don't think I like it. I don't like how I'm not confident around you. But keeping the honesty thing alive, I am super attracted to you. Like seriously, not a hair out of place." I finished.

Trent smiled and he really listened to me. "You're one in a million Dee baby. Sal is right, no one will ever be good enough for you. You deserve so much. But, to get the kind of love that lasts Dee baby, you have to put yourself out there and be vulnerable. Give it time. I'll be waiting on you and caring about you in the meantime."

Then the elevator dinged and Doc walked out. Saved by the Doc. The conversation was getting extremely too tense.

"Good morning Trent and good morning Dee. You're looking much better today." He said smiling through his round lensed glasses.

"I feel much better. Thank you for all you did for me. I appreciate it." I said.

"I'm just doing my job. Let me take this IV out and check your head and you should be good to go." He said moving towards my IV arm.

Trent watched closely as Doc worked. He pulled the IV out and put a band aid on my arm. Then he walked around to my back and turned my head down and pushed my hair out of the way so he could look at my head where the bump was. He pushed around it and it made me see stars.

"It looks ok. You got a concussion and the swelling messed with your vison and motor movement last night, but it was so bad, partly, because you were dehydrated. Today drink plenty of water and apple juice if you want. Also, Ibuprofen for your head. It will be tender for several days. Other than that, you're completely ok," said Doc.

Trent walked Doc back to the elevator and handed him several bills out of his wallet. I watched as the two exchanged words and then Doc grabbed Trent's arm in a kind squeeze and he was gone. I got up, holding the robe closed as I bent down to the bags on the floor. There were four bags full of brand new, designer clothes. I had never had anything so nice or new. I picked up a leather jacket. I loved it. It looked bad ass. Like biker chick bad ass. Like I drive a muscle car bad ass. I dropped it and sat on my butt and cried.

Trent came over to me really worried. "Dee baby, if you don't like the clothes I'll go buy you whatever you want."

I shook my head. "I love the clothes."

Poor Trent looked so confused, "Then, I'm not sure what the problem is. If it's not the clothes..." He trailed off.

"It is the clothes. Not that I don't like them. I can't afford anything like this. I never could. These are the first brand name, new clothes I've ever gotten. I'm eighteen and I've never had anything that was just for me. Thank you. They are bad ass." I said through sniffles.

Trent grabbed me by my shoulders, "I'll buy you whatever brand new clothes you want. I can do that for you. I owe you for being so good about everything. And Lilian wasn't lying, I do get a family discount at the boutique, but I'll buy you clothes from anywhere you want. You deserve at least that Dee baby. Go try on your new bad ass clothes and model for me."

I smiled and whispered, "Ok."

I grabbed my bags and went to his room and dumped the clothes out on the big bed. There were shorts, jeans, dresses, blouses, T-shirts, and then I saw them, knee high, black leather, high heel, boots. I knew what I wanted to wear today.

Trent looked up when I walked out of his room and he let out a whistle. I had on tight jeans with my new knee-high boots, a white skin tight blouse with a v cut out over the top of my chest to just show a hint of cleavage, and the bad ass, black leather jacket. I had brushed my hair out and made it big. I didn't have any makeup with me, so I had to go natural, but I would of killed for some black eyeliner and red lipstick.

"Damn Dee baby. You look sexy." Trent said.

I couldn't help but smile. "Somehow I think you had a hand in this outfit," I said.

Trent shrugged and said, "I may have mention a leather jacket and boots. I could picture you in Fiona in a leather jacket."

I ran over to him and hugged his neck. He was surprised. He reached around and hugged me back.

"I'm glad you like it Dee. That smile on your face is worth it all." He said.

"I've never had anything this nice and it feels surreal to me Trent. I'm not used to this. And all the other clothes in there your sister picked are amazing. She has good taste. Which brings me to the next thing…It looks like the boutique threw up on your bed. Do you have a guest room for me? I'll clean the clothes out there and be out of your hair." I said.

He looked a little disappointed that I asked about another room, but we were just friends. We may have slept in the same bed last night, but I was in no condition to be on my own.

He nodded and said, "I'll help you get your stuff there when we get back. Now I think we need to go take care of Sal's stuff."

I stiffened. I was so excited for new clothes, I had forgotten what was really important. I nodded and said, "You're right. I'm driving."

He smiled and said, "I'd have it no other way. One thing before we leave."

Trent disappeared into his room and came out with a pair of aviator sunglasses and handed them to me and he had another pair for himself. "I think these will look good with your jacket."

I smiled at him. When he wasn't bashing girls over the head, he was actually pretty sweet.

Chapter 12

I was real fidgety as I drove Fiona to Sal's. I was anxious. Trent watched me closely. He could tell I was just barely hanging on. When I pulled into the shop/gas station, Sally was there. She was inside working. The show must go on. People still needed gas and what else was she to do?

A group of kids I went to school with watched as I pulled Fiona in. When I parked her and got out, the shock registered on their faces, and their mouths actually dropped open when they saw Trent come around and grab my hand. I let him, because I needed all the support I could get to face Sal being gone.

"Dee is that you?" A blonde girl named Cher asked. She was a cheerleader.

I just nodded and kept walking. They weren't my friends.

"You're not going to introduce us to the hot guy with you?" She asked batting her eyebrows.

"No." I curtly answered and kept walking.

There was no sense in them pretending to know I existed now because I'm with a hot guy and have new clothes on.

"Dee that's not very nice." Cher continued to speak.

"Cher I don't have time for this today. I have a funeral to plan and things to see to. Some of us have to be adults." I spat out at her and turned and didn't look back.

Trent waved bye to them and chuckled. "Tell her how you really feel." He said.

"You have no idea." I said back.

Sally looked up when I walked in and her eyes registered shock as she saw Trent with me. I let go of his hand and went around the counter and hugged her tight.

"Are you ok Dee?" She asked searching my face. "You ran off last night and I was worried when you didn't come in this morning and I hadn't gotten a chance to get your cell. I thought you might need some time alone."

"I'm really not ok, but I will be. Sal wouldn't let me be anything less. I'm sorry I took off without saying anything. I was in a bad state last night. Luckily, Trent showed up and literally held my hand through the night."

Trent twitched at that and Sally looked at him closely.

"Well then Trent, I'm glad you were there for her. Dee is a special girl and she needs someone strong in her corner," said Sally. She then asked, "Dee I thought you never spoke to him again after he came in here that day. You were holding out on me. I told you he looked at you like he wanted to taste you." And she laughed.

"Sally!" I shrieked.

Trent busted out laughing.

I broke the light moment, "Sally I'm going to head to the funeral home. They were supposed to take Sal there this morning. Do you think there's anything I need to say or do that I may not think of?"

She shook her head, "Dee you were the most important thing in his life. Whatever you say or decide will be what he wanted."

I hugged her again, grabbed one of my suckers, and went back out to Fiona to head to the funeral home. Trent opened my door for me and went around and got in. The group of kids were still there watching us. I started Fiona up and gave her a little more gas than necessary. I wanted to feel her move. Trent got a wicked grin on his face when I put her in gear.

I made it over to the funeral home. I turned Fiona off and sat looking at the building for a long time. Trent studied me. He grabbed one of my hands that was tightly gripping the steering wheel and placed it to his mouth and kissed it. I looked at him. I could feel the tears prickling my eyes. I took a deep breath and said, "Now or never."

We got out and walked into the funeral home. Mr. Baker was the director. He knew Sal and I personally. We did all of his service on his personal vehicles and the work related ones as well. His eyes warmed when he saw me walk in.

"Dee. I figured you'd be in today. How ya holding up sweetheart?" Mr. Baker asked.

"To be honest, not well. I loved Ol' Sal. Mr. Baker you're going to have to help me through this. I'm not sure what all I need to do." I told him.

He smiled softly at me and said, "I know sweetheart. I'll help you with everything."

Two hours later, everything was figured out. Sal had life insurance so the funeral was covered. I had to pick his coffin. I picked a sparkly blue one and asked Mr. Baker if I could come back before he was put in there to add white racing stripes. Mr. Baker nodded his approval. I would make sure his coffin was as close to Betty as I could get it. We had his newspaper write up done, the obituary done, and I had even ran to his house to get clothes for him to wear. I got him a pair of his Dickies coveralls of course. That's how everyone knew Sal and I knew he would want to leave the way he always was. I also grabbed his oily, old, feed store cap.

After a quiet lunch with Trent at the only diner in town, I went to the paint garage and got some white paint, tape, and some regular brushes, and clear coat. I also went into Sal's house and changed into old jeans and a Lynard Skynard t-shirt. Trent looked at me and smiled. My clothes were still there. I took one of Sal's old work trucks back up to the funeral home. I was not going to put paint in Fiona or get back in Fiona after painting.

Trent rode with me back up to the funeral home. Mr. Baker led me to a side room that he said I could use to paint the stripes on the coffin. He left Trent and I to it, because he had another grieving family coming in to consult. I laid out the drop cloth and rolled the coffin in place. I taped off two, perfect racing stripes. I tied my hair up in a messy bun on top of my head and opened the paint. I picked up a brush, but my hands were shaking. I just stared at my hands and started to hyperventilate.

"Dee baby. Look at me. It's going to be ok. Breathe baby. You don't have to paint that stripe on there. It'll be ok," said Trent.

"It's not ok. Sal is gone. I have to paint the stripes. I have too. He will never drive Betty again. I need to do this. This is for Sal. I guess painting on his coffin means I'm accepting it. I can't accept he's gone." I said in a really thick voice that was cracking.

Trent looked at me and nodded in understanding. "Well, how about I paint the stripes? I'm sure I can manage. You can watch me and make sure I do it right." He said.

I shook my head no. "I've got to do this. I've got to pull myself together and do this." I took a really deep breath and shook my hands out.

I picked up a brush, dipped it, and slowly and very carefully I started to fill in my stripes in between the strips of tape. Thank God for tape today. I let the tears fall as the stripes became clear and full. I didn't wipe my eyes. I let them hit the ground and kept stroking the brush to fill in the stripes. When I finished putting the white stripes on, I sat back and looked. They would work and his coffin would have a bit of Betty on it. I felt strong arms wrap around me from behind. Trent was there. He was literally holding me up in this moment. I don't know if he realized just how much I needed him to hold me right then. Sal was gone and this made it real.

I let the white completely dry and then Trent helped me pull the tape off. The stripes looked even and full. I smiled at them. I then, clear coated them. I heard Sal telling me not to "half ass my job." When, I had finished, I stepped back and looked. It was no Betty, but it looked like Sal. Mr. Baker told me not to worry about the drop cloth and that he would pick it up in the morning. The paint need to dry for 12 hours. Trent drove the work truck back to Sal's and put everything up and I went back in his house and changed back into my new clothes.

"The viewing and funeral is in three days. Do you want to come the day before and stay the night here so you can tie up loose ends?" Trent asked.

"That sounds like a smart plan. It will give me time to process things and get my head together. I don't know how to leave this behind." I said looking at Trent and wondering why in the world he was sticking with me for all of this. I guess that twenty large is a big deal for him.

"Do you want me to drive home?" He asked me.

"It's been a long day, but Fiona is calling my name. I need to get her on the open road and feel her horses run." I said.

Trent smiled at me and said, "I think you're going to be ok."

Chapter 13

Trent talked to his father about our plan to have me fix up some old cars for him to get his money back. Giorgio said that for his son and for me, he would spend some money to make some. That meant, though, I would have to get his twenty thousand plus whatever it cost him to buy cars and parts. It was doable and it was way better than them putting Fiona up for sale.

The next evening, Trent and I went to his parent's house for dinner. I was nervous and it felt odd to me to be included on family things. Lilian had told his mom about me and she insisted that Trent bring his girlfriend to dinner. I wasn't sure what to do. I never corrected Lilian and for some reason I felt the need to protect Trent from his sister when she had come to the penthouse. I didn't tell her the truth of the bump on my head or that he really had no clue if I was in fact, velvet.

Trent said, "I'll tell them you are sick if you don't want to go, but Ma will just keep inviting us until you come. I've never had a woman staying with me and she's anxious to meet the girl that caught my attention."

"But, I really didn't want to stay here. I won't ruin your mom's idea of her precious son, but we are not a couple. I don't know why I let Lilian believe that. I should have corrected her. I think I was just in shock with the conversation and clothes."

"Yeah I'm still sorry about that, but speaking of clothes…Why do you still have all the tags on your dresser?" He asked.

"I plan on paying you back after I settle my father's debt with your father. I told you I don't want a handout and if I'm here for work fine, but I can't just accept extravagant gifts from you." I explained.

Trent looked at me and let out a deep sigh and marched passed me. He headed into the guest room, that I was now staying in, because under no circumstances was I going to sleep in the same bed with him again.

"What are you doing Trent?" I questioned him.

He didn't answer. He walked right into my room, grabbed the tags off the dresser, and promptly threw them away. "I told you. I owed you for that. I will not accept your money for something I owed you and wanted to do. It's ok to accept gifts from someone. Not everyone expects something in return." He finally said.

I just looked at him. I had nothing to say to that. It was true I didn't know how to just accept a gift. I thought about Sal always finding a way to make it seem like what he was giving me benefited him. He knew I was fragile and had a bad mentality because of Brian. I would have kept my mouth shut, had Trent not said something else.

"Your money is no good here anyway." He said without thinking.

I turned red and let my anger spew," If my money is no good here, then why the hell am I staying here to work off a debt that isn't even mine. God you're such a contradicting ass. I think I like you for one minute and this may not be so bad, to wanting to throttle you in the next. You drive me insane!"

Trent rubbed the back of his neck. "Yeah I could see how that last thing I said wouldn't go over well. I said it without thinking. I'm sorry. Your money is no good to me. Twenty thousand dollars is a lot and that isn't owed to me, it's owed to my Pop. That's different. I'm sorry. I promise I'll try to think before I speak. You mess me up Dee baby. I can't hide that I like you and damn it, I'm excited to eat dinner with my family and pretend your mine. I want you to be mine."

I just looked at him. I was mad, confused, sad, and a multitude of other feelings. Trent's words were always so brazen. I almost wanted to let go of all the bad and give him a chance, but I was scared. I didn't want to back door a horrible time in my life with a bad decision.

I went to my room and got ready to go dinner. I wasn't sure what to wear. I had never felt the need to dress up for anything, because I never had reason to or anywhere to go. I opted for a fitted red dress. It had small sleeves and a square neck line. It was classy and definitely something you would wear to meet parents. I, however, had already met Giorgio and was nervous about seeing him again. I wore my hair down and straightened it. I put just mascara on and lip gloss. Lilian had also brought me shoes. I found a pair of nude wedges and went with those. They made my legs look long.

I walked out of my room feeling pretty good about myself. The saying that a good pair of shoes can make a woman ready to take on the world, could very well be true. Trent was waiting for me at the bar with a pair of khakis on and a white polo shirt and brown loafers with a brown belt. He looked like an ivy league guy. I smiled at him.

"Dee, you look beautiful. Ma is going to love you and Lilian will flip over how good you look in the clothes she picked for you. C'mon let's go." Trent said.

We went down to the garage and got into Tammy. That orange beauty could really go. I tried not to act too excited to be riding in her, but Trent already knew. Tammy was a sexy car. I smiled when he hit the gas and I noted how high her RPM's went as he shifted gears. I loved the sound of her. I had my eyes closed listening to her purr, when I opened them to see Trent staring at me.

"What?" I asked him feeling a little embarrassed.

"You are totally loving Tammy. I can see your wheels turning as you listen to her and the smile that plays at the corner of your lips is a giveaway. You love my car. " Trent said teasing, but I saw something else in his eyes, longing, maybe.

"So? I like nice cars that go fast and purr like a cat. I know Tammy is nice. I've seen her insides. I could make her faster though by playing with her torque." I said thinking out loud.

"I wish you thought of me with the same look you have on your face when you're thinking about cars," said Trent with a sad smile.

My eyes softened as I looked at him, "I think I may want to look at you that way. But I'm not sure I can. I've got a lot going on right now and I feel like I should tackle one thing at a time."

Trent got a huge smile on his face and mine went immediately hot.

"Oh my gosh! I can't believe I just said that out loud." I groaned.

"All I needed to know is I have a chance Dee baby," said Trent still smiling.

I looked out the window trying to avoid his gaze.

We pulled up to a mansion of a home. It had the black iron type fence all around it and a keypad at the gate that had a calligraphy T on it. The home itself was breath taking. It was stone on the outside and you could tell it was old by the way the stones were laid. The landscaping was gorgeous. They had yaupon holly bushes groomed to look like spirals. They had lights shining up in all the trees. It was like a magical fairy garden. It was breath taking and that was just the outside.

"Trent this home, it's gorgeous. You grew up here?" I asked with bright eyes.

"I sure did. I was blessed. I had a great childhood." He said in a gentle way. I could tell he was trying to protect me from what mine was.

He pulled in and parked next to a fancy SUV. "That's Lilian's car. She bought it when she found out she was pregnant." Trent said.

We walked up to the big front door and it swung wide open before we even touched the door and I was being pulled into a hug by a short, olive skinned woman with red lipstick on. Dang. The women in this family were huggers. I was shocked at first and then just hugged her back.

"Ma! C'mon. She doesn't even know you," said Trent.

"Oh Giorgie that's because you haven't introduced us yet." His mom said.

"You didn't exactly give me time to. You just swung the door open and grabbed my girl." Trent said and then he said, "Ma this is Dee. Dee this is Ma."

I looked up with my eyebrows raised and said, "Hello nice to meet you?"

"Oh call me Ma. That's what all the kids call me and you will be no different," said Ma.

I smiled and said, "Ok then, Ma."

She nodded her approval and said, "Silly me! C'mon in guys!"

"What am I chopped liver Ma? You hug Dee and leave me hanging." Trent said acting insulted.

"Oh my Giorgie come here!" She said acting like it was a big deal.

I smiled at the exchange. Ma then took my hand and ushered me in. I was taken aback when I walked through the door. There was a huge crystal chandelier hanging in the foyer and a spiral stair case with polished cherry wood rails just to the right. It was a brilliant white when you came in. She ushered us to the dining area. It smelled wonderful.

"It smells amazing. I'm excited to eat. Do you need me to help you with anything?" I asked Ma.

She gave me a warm smile. "You are precious. I've got it all done. Come in and meet everyone else and tell Lilian hi. She's been going on and on about you. She said you were really nice." Ma said.

I smiled and followed. Trent was close on my heels. I walked into the elegant dining room. The walls were a tan with warm browns and warm lights along the walls. There was a large table in the middle with food all along the middle of the table. Sitting at the head of the table was Giorgio on his left was Lilian, a high chair, and a man who I assumed was her husband. Trent took his seat at the right side of his father and nodded his head at me to the seat next to him. I moved to take my seat and Ma sat at the other end of the table facing Giorgio.

"Oh I just love having a full table! Everyone this is Trent's beautiful girlfriend, Dee. Dee you know Lilian already. That's her husband Stephen and baby girl Haley and at the head of the table is Giorgio, my handsome husband and my kids' Pop. So as you know you are to call me Ma and I'm sure you'll know that we expect you to call him Pop. We are family here and family comes first. Before long you'll have a nickname too." Ma said smiling at me and you could see how proud she was of her family.

I nodded and took it all in. Giorgio was studying me. I looked him in the eye and said, "Nice to meet you Pop." And I may have emphasize Pop a little more than necessary. He smiled real big at me and I heard Trent suppress a chuckle.

Giorgio, I mean Pop, spoke up, "Let's say grace so we can dig into this wonderful meal your Ma prepared." I was taken aback when Trent grabbed one of my hands and Ma the other.

Then, he prayed, "Dear Heavenly Father,

We thank you for the bounty in front of us and the family beside us. You provide for us above and beyond what we need and we thank you for it. We thank you for our growing family and new bonds being made and I pray you guide and protect us all and let this food go to the nourishment of our bodies.

In your mighty name,

Amen"

Everyone chorused amen and the food started getting passed around. Ma had made her famous lasagna, garlic bread knots, Brussel sprouts, and corn. It was a feast and so good.

"Ma this food tastes even better than it smells. Thank you for cooking for us. Will you please give me the recipe so I can make this at home?" I asked.

Trent's eyebrows shot up.

Ma beamed with delight. "You are most welcome Dee. I'm so happy you like it. I'll do you one better, you can come over the next time I make it and I'll show you. I make the noodles from scratch too."

"Wow! I knew these noodles were something special," I said as I took another bite and groaning in ecstasy.

Pop spoke up then, "We like a girl that's not afraid to enjoy her food." He chuckled.

"Then I'm your girl. I love food." I said actually smiling at him.

He was so much different tonight than the first time I met him. Little Haley was enjoying her food too and making a big mess in the process. She had tomato sauce over her entire face. I was smiling watching her and she noticed me, so I made a silly face at her and she started laughing. Unfortunately, I forgot that I was at a table with adults and I made Lilian laugh too.

I blushed.

Lilian busted in, "Don't be embarrassed! You should see what Uncle Giorgie does to win a giggle. You look great in that dress by the way."

"Thanks. This really cool girl who knows her fashion picked it out for me," I said winking at her.

"Oh yes! You have to be my sister!" Squealed Lilian.

Stephen was more quiet. I guessed Lilian did all the talking. He gave me a warm smile when I continued to make faces across the table at Haley. It made me happy to hear her giggle. I kept feeling Trent stare at me, but I tried to ignore it. The dinner was nice. It was full of laughter and a family that really cared about one another. I wasn't used to this and I realized I had missed a lot growing up. I took it in and it seemed to be overwhelming at times.

When we finished eating, Ma started to clear the dishes. I got up and immediately helped her. "Dee go sit back down. You're our guest," she hissed at me.

"No ma'am. I won't. You cooked a five star meal. There's no way I'm letting you clean up by yourself." I told her.

"Giorgie, you better marry this girl, " she hollered from the kitchen.

I heard the laughter from the table and I thought for but a moment that being part of this family might be something special. Lilian walked into the kitchen with a dirty Haley. She took her over to the sink and washed her up and handed her to me saying, "Here you play with Haley and I'll help Ma get the dishes rinsed and in the washer."

I took the little two year old happily. I always loved kids and her and I bonded over faces at the table. She slapped my chest and I laughed and called her a, "little toot." I started singing Twinkle Twinkle Little Star and dancing around the kitchen with her, making her laugh.

"You're a natural with a baby Dee," said Ma.

I smiled still twirling and said, "I'm good at goofy. Thanks. I love kids."

"Good I want to be an aunt one day," said Lilian.

I felt my heart stutter. I wasn't even really Trent's girlfriend and they were making plans that involved me. I felt bad for leading them on, but there was no way I could tell these two wonderful women the truth of how we come to be together all the time. I kept dancing with Haley and then stopped to blow raspberries on her tummy and she laughed so hard. I turned to see Trent standing in the doorway, legs crossed, leaning against it, smiling at me. He was watching me and he had a look in his eyes I couldn't register. They were soft, but there was something else there.

"Trent why don't you take Dee out to the back porch. You know Haley loves to rock in the swing back there. Dee will love the porch too," Ma said over her shoulder from the sink.

"Ok Ma. Come on Dee. Let's take Haley to swing," said Trent smiling at his niece.

Apparently she knew the word swing, because she got excited and starting bouncing on my hip and squealing. Trent grabbed my hand that wasn't holding a bouncing toddler and led me outside through a back door to a beautiful porch overlooking a big yard full of more lit trees. There were pot plants everywhere and lights and a little water fountain and in the corner, a wooden porch swing.

We went and sat down on the swing. It seemed normal. We just played with Haley and gently pushed back and forth. Trent was tickling her and calling her Boo Baby. Haley was eating it up.

"Your Uncle Giorgie is silly." I said in a goofy baby voice.

She clapped her hands.

"Can you say Dee?" I asked her.

She clapped her hands some more. I laughed.

"Say Dee." I said poking her belly.

"You better not say Dee before Giorgie," said Trent teasing.

She laughed and then slapped my chest, giggled, and said, "DEEEEEE!"

I was so happy I laughed and said, "Yay smart girl. That's right. I'm Dee."

"No, say Giorgie! Giorgieeee!" Said Trent.

She clapped her hands and said, "DEEEEEEEE!!!" again.

It was now a game, so I said, "Wahooo!! That's right baby girl! DEEEEE!" And I tickled her.

"Oh man. I'm so heart broken. She's met you one time and says your name and I buy her toys and play with her all the time…." Trent acted like he was so sad.

"Poor Uncle Giorgie. He doesn't understand that us chicks have to stick together. Haley girl, can you say Giorgie?" I asked her poking her uncle and making him yelp.

She laughed and poked him. He yelped for her too.

So I poked him in the ribs and said, "My Giorgie."

Haley looked at me funny and poked his ribs and said, "My Orgie."

I busted out laughing. "Oh yes Haley girl. You and I are besties now. Sorry Orgie."

I heard a laugh from the back door. Giorgio was standing there watching us. I wondered how long he had been there. I hadn't noticed. I did notice, however, that I called Haley, Haley girl. Sal always called me Dee girl. My heart clenched. I wanted to cry. I felt guilty for having such a good time when Sal hadn't even been gone long.

I was broke from my melancholy when Haley hit my chest and said, "Deeeee!" And then she poked Trent's ribs and said, "My Orgieeee!!"

"That's right Haley girl," I snickered, "My Orgie."

Trent gave me a look and then said, "Well at least she calls me hers, but technically you called me your Giorgie first, sooo….."

I shot a look back at him and he laughed and whispered, "I have a chance."

I hadn't realized his arm was around my shoulder until that moment. I guess it had been there the whole time. Haley nestled in between us and rested her head on my side and fell asleep giggling. We gently pushed the swing back and forth for a long time.

Chapter 14

"Giorgie, why don't you go lay Haley down," Giorgio told him.

Trent nodded and carefully grabbed Haley and took her inside. I got up and walked over to the railing and looked out over the yard. Giorgio came up next to me. I tensed. I wasn't sure how this was going to go. Besides Trent and I, he was the only other one that knew what the whole truth was.

He spoke after a moment, "My family loves ya Dee darlin'. You fit in well here. I have to ask ya, why didn't you tell Lilian the truth of what happened when she stopped by the other day?"

I sighed, "To be honest, I'm not sure. She just seemed to love him so much and I could tell she thinks he walks on water. I didn't want to mess that up for either of them. She was so nice to me and I liked her right off the bat, even if she is a bit forward."

He chuckled at that. "That she is. And tonight? You came and said not a word. You acted like you are really just here with Giorgie."

"I've never had a family and to see yours sit to dinner and laugh together and be happy... I just couldn't be the one to mess that up, even if you and your son deserve to be thrown under the bus." I said calmly, even though I felt anything but calm.

"You're still fired up I see. I don't blame ya. But I also ain't blind. I see the way my son looks at you. It's the same way I look at my Marge. I also have noticed you glancing at him. I can see why you wouldn't want to be involved with him after everything, but he's a good man. A real partner is hard to find, so when you find one you hold on to em." He said.

"Mr. Giorgio and are you a good man? I see you're a wonderful family man, but do they not know you have goons doing dirty work for you? I like the version of you here, but I'm about to work off twenty grand for my father, when it's not even my debt. How does that sit with you? How should it sit with me, that your son is on board for me to work off something that I had no part in to begin with?" I asked of him.

He studied me for a long time and took a deep breath. Giorgio then said, "Call me Pop. You heard Ma. You are going to be around a lot in foreseeable future and I think I'll like you to call me Pop. You're real brassy kid. I like you a lot and I could help you grow in your business. You don't have to work it off for me. I'm out twenty thousand dollars though. You'd be doing me a favor if you stuck around and helped me recover that. I saw your car. She's beautiful and someone that can do work like that and fix something that couldn't run to start with, has a real shot in life to run a business. My family really likes you and my son cares for you, so as a Pop, I'm going to ask you stick around. You have my word you will be safe with us and I'll tell Giorgie to keep you out of any business that you may not like and we will quit holding you accountable for Brian's misdeeds."

I let a single tear fall down my cheek and Pop swiped it off with a thumb. "I know everything Dee darlin. Giorgie and I don't keep secrets from one another. I can imagine what it feels like to be around us after losing your dad. Sal was a good man from what I understand. I'm sorry darlin. I'm sorry you feel alone. You don't have to be though. Giorgie wants to be there for you and I saw a whole table who will have your back if you let them." He then wrapped me in a bear hug. I was taken aback. I didn't expect him to be so tender to me, let alone hug me.

I clung to him and wept. I wept for the kindness, for Sal, for the family that let me be a part of them if only for one evening, and for the promise of someone keeping me safe.

He rubbed my head and said, "You don't have to be alone kid. It's ok let it out, so you can be strong later. No more running or hiding." I could tell me showing him my true feelings meant something to him.

I finished crying and squeezed him harder. Only a dad could hug like that. I pulled away and looked up at him and nodded and said, "I'll stay to help you out and because now, I know Haley likes me more than Trent."

Pop's mouth quirked into a smile and I smiled back. "We will be glad to have ya kid. Go a little easier on Giorgie. He's new to having real feelings."

I laughed and nodded. I turned to see there was an audience watching us through the glass doors. When I walked in, Ma and Lilian both pulled me into a giant hug together. I was sandwiched in between them and I didn't mind at all.

Ma said, "We are sorry about you dad dear. You need anything, you let us know. We are here for you. You are not alone."

There it was again. I wasn't alone. I smiled and nodded at her.

"Dee you're part of this family now, whether you like it or not!" said Lilian.

"I think I like it Lilian. Especially since Haley can say Dee and that she calls her uncle My Orgie." I said busting out laughing.

Everyone else erupted into laughter.

"She called him Orgie?!" Lilian shrieked.

"Yes. I got her to say Dee and then tried to get her to say Giorgie, but she's definitely calling him Orgie," I said belly laughing.

"It's true. I heard it with my own two ears," said Pop chuckling.

"Ha. Very funny guys. At least my name is action packed," said Trent rocking his hips.

Ma hit him with a towel. We all sat in the family room sipping coffee and visiting some more. Ma wanted to know all about me. She was so upset to hear about my biological father and how Sal died. She definitely was mortified when she heard how I grew up essentially alone and trying to figure out how to buy groceries and keep myself safe. They all wanted to know how Trent and I met, so we stuck with shop story. Stephen finally spoke up when he heard I could work on cars. He had an old Porsche that was his grandfather's that didn't run. I promised I would look it over. Pop filled them in that I would be helping him to raise some money by working on cars and that I was doing him a big favor. We finally said our goodbyes and Ma saw us off with leftovers and told me she would be calling me soon to come over to learn how to make her lasagna.

We got into Tammy and Trent turned and looked at me and said, "Dee you know you're amazing right? My whole family loves you, even Pop. He told me what happened on the back porch. You are so brave. He respects you. Thank you."

"Thank you for what?" I asked.

"For deciding to stay." He said and squeezed my leg.

"It's my pleasure Orgie." I said laughing.

"You ain't right!" He shouted towards the sky.

I just laughed. "It's pretty right. You deserve all you get," I said.

"Touché." He said.

He put the car in drive and we went out of the fancy gate and I found myself sad to leave. We were quiet for most of the way back to the penthouse. Trent spoke up, "Why are you so wonderful? You had every right to tell Ma and Lilian what really happened, even if I didn't mean it to. You could be pissed at the world for the hand you were dealt and no one would blame you."

I didn't have an answer. I just looked at him and shrugged my shoulders. I thought for a few minutes and then finally came up with an answer. "Trent I am pissed if I'm honest. I'm pissed that I could be born to two horrible people. I'm pissed I never had family dinners or the love like I just experienced with your family. I'm pissed that I had to grow up so fast and worry about bills and food from such  a young age. With that being said, I was also loved by Sal in his own way. He gave me a job, a purpose and I took it to heart. He gave me friendship and soft words when I needed them. I may not have had good parents to be an example for me, but I had an example of what I didn't want to be like. I tried to be the complete opposite. I had school and took every opportunity to learn as much as I could. I never missed a field trip. Sal always made sure of that. So yeah, I got dealt a shitty hand, but I had a king among the jokers. Sometimes all you need is one person to believe in you. "

He looked at me with soft eyes and then asked again, "And Ma and Lilian? You never told them."

I looked away and spoke out the window. "I would never be the reason to cause a happy family to be anything but that. I really like your mom and sister and if I'm being honest, your dad too. The family man side of him is warm and loving. I saw the family photos. I saw your dad as your baseball coach and dressed in a tux with Lilian for a dance. I saw anniversary photos of your parents and how happy they were and I couldn't ruin that. I see how your mom and sister adore you and I couldn't hurt them in that way, or you. I don't want to hurt you either."

"I'm on a rollercoaster of emotions with you. You've seen me at my absolute worst. Sure you caused that worst, but I heard what you said. I felt your gentle care. I've noticed how you make sure I have everything I could possibly need or even want before I ask. I see the way you are with your niece. I don't want to like you, but I do." I said still not looking at him.

I could feel his gaze on me. I just put myself out there and I wasn't ready to see how he received it. I wasn't ready for the heaviness of this situation. I had a lot to sort out in my own mind. And as if he could read me, he said, "Well if all it took was getting my niece to call me Orgie, I would have done that a long time ago."

I started laughing and then whispered, "Thank you."

He just nodded. I think he understood why I said it.

Chapter 15

We were headed back to Sal's in Tammy. Trent insisted on driving. He said he wanted me to only have to worry about getting through the next two days and didn't want me to be driving while I was worried about the funeral. After, our family dinner, things were a little weird. Neither one of us really knew how to act towards the other. I had told him I liked him. He didn't push for anything. Our relationship was tense. We weren't really friends but we weren't a couple either. Yet, he was right by my side for the roughest thing I'd ever had to go through. I kept wondering if I should try to let him in, but I was scared of my own feelings.

We made it to Sal's. I had plans to get my things loaded from his house, grab his coffee cup, that would be mine, and get some of the posters off the wall and the Jeff Gordon throw. I knew he wouldn't care. I also needed to get my tools from the garage. I went into the shop and saw Sally was there working. People still needed gas in the small town. I wondered how the town would get along after everything. So much was in limbo. Sal was the only mechanic garage/gas station in town. I wasn't sure what would happen.

"Hey Sally," I said as I went around the counter to hug her.

"Dee. I've been missing you. It's so quiet around here without you and Sal working on cars," said Sally.

I took a ragged breath and said, "I know. My life seems too quiet without him."

"Nice to see you again Trent." Sally said looking him over.

"You too Sally. I wish I was here for a happier reason." Trent said looking at me.

Then, the bell over the door dinged and a little, old lady walked in. I immediately recognized her as Ms. Darla, our town's crazy cat lady. After her husband died, she took it upon herself to feed all the stray cats in our town. She would ride out to back roads and out to abandoned places to feed them. I smiled at her and so did Sally.

"Hi Ms. Darla. Do you need help getting anything today?" Sally asked.

"I just don't know what to do without Sal here to fix my car. It wouldn't start and then I got it to start finally and I'm scared to turn it off. If I can't drive, the cats will be hungry." She said with her face full of worry.

"Well, we can't have that. I won't allow it and plus Sal would be mad at me if I didn't help you out. Ms. Darla, I'm sure I can figure it out for you. Let me go change into some work clothes and I'll fix your car right up. You just sit in here with Sally." I said straightening up. I had to help her. Sal would have.

"I'm just going to leave the keys in it running dear. I'm afraid if I turn it off, it won't start again." She said.

"That's fine. I'll only be a moment and I'll drive the car into Bay one and see what I can do," I said turning on my heel to walk out the back door and get to Sal's house.

Trent followed me. He didn't say a word. I got Sal's spare key out from under the rock in the flowerbed and let myself in. I went straight to my room and put on a pair of old jeans and a white T-shirt. I had a purpose today and I needed it. I could pack posters later.

"Do you want some help?" Trent asked.

I raised my eyebrows and said, "Do you know how to work on cars?"

"I know my way around them and I'm a quick study, " said Trent.

"Ok. Then come on. You can at least be good for handing me tools," I teased.

We got back to the garage and I opened bay one and had Trent pull the old, Lincoln town car in. I could tell by the sound of the car she was missing. I ran through in my head all the possibilities; bad starter, plugged fuel line, and so on. I told Trent to pop the hood and I got to work. Before I had been working ten minutes another car pulled in.

Sally hollered through the side door, "Honey you opened a garage door, now everyone who needs anything vehicle related will be showing up."

I looked at Trent and shrugged my shoulders. "That's fine Sally. Just get the clipboards worked up for me, so I know what I'm looking at. I get to all I can today."

Trent smiled and walked off into the store. When he came back, he was holding two cherry Tootsie Pops. I smiled at him. I looked to my hands, which were dirty and working on the car in front of me. Trent got the picture, because he unwrapped the sucker for me and slowly put it in my mouth. I think he enjoyed that way too much, but I wasn't going to complain. He went and got me one without me having to ask.

I got Ms. Darla fixed up. It was a blocked fuel line. Easy fix. Ms. Darla was so happy she hugged me even though I was dirty. No cats would be hungry on my watch.  I got Trent to open up the second bay door and pull the next vehicle in. This one needed an oil change. Easy enough. I got to work. I had Trent clean windows and put the new oil change sticker on for me. Another car showed up, it needed an AC charge. I felt Trent's eyes on me as I worked. I knew I was filthy. Working cars on had a way of doing that. I had dirt and grease smudges on my shirt and my hands were black.

Trent kept my suckers coming and the cherry cokes. The only thing was he only got one big cherry coke, so we were sharing. I felt a little funny about it, but oh well. Before I knew it, it was five o clock and I had put in a full workday in Sal's garage. It was bitter sweet. This would be my last day in this garage to work. As I closed down the last bay door, I let my head rest on it. My emotions were heavy. Sally opened the side door and hollered, "Honey it's past five. You need to get out of here and get some rest."

I knew she was ready to leave so I hollered back, "I know. I need to clean up a little in here. Go ahead home Sally. I'll lock up."

"Ok honey. See you tomorrow. You did good today." She said.

I still had my head on the bay door and was taking a deep breath, when I heard Trent's footsteps slowly coming up behind me. I turned around and rested my back against the door with my head tilted back on it. He studied me. I thought about all the good memories I had in here with Sal. I thought about the first day he brought me in here and started teaching me which tools were what. I thought about the first oil change I did by myself and the endless hours we spent together solving the world's problems under the hood of a car. I let a single tear fall and hit the dirty garage floor.

"Dee baby. Are you ok? I know today was a lot for you. You were amazing going from car to car. Sal would be proud of how you commanded his garage today, " said Trent in a soft voice.

I smiled at him. "I'm ok. I was just thinking of all the happy memories I have in here. Pretty much all my good memories are here. There are so many. I thought for so long I had such a sad excuse of a life and no good childhood memories, but I do. They just involve being dirty and working in this garage. I want to make one last good memory in here. Trent would you help me do that?"

He took a step closer and said, "I would love nothing more than to help you make a happy memory. I don't know if you noticed, but I'd do just about anything for you Dee baby."

I nodded, believing him and then I just asked what I wanted his help with, "Will you give me my first real kiss? Not like at your place, but a real one. One that I want. I want you to give me my first kiss right here in this garage."

Trent looked at me and walked the rest of the distance slowly towards me. He put his hand at the base of my head and grabbed my hair and wrapped his other arm around my waist and pulled me flush to him. He ran his nose down mine and looked deep into my eyes. I pressed into him and he slowly and gently pressed his lips to mine. He backed just barely away, with our noses still touching and searched my eyes. He then closed the gap and kissed me again, more passionately and this time when he parted his lips, I did too and I let him have my mouth. Our tongues glided along one another, deepening our kiss. He kissed me for a long time before he stopped. My chest was heaving and my mouth tingled. I loved it.

"I was right," he said smiling with his forehead pressed against mine.

"Right about what?" I asked.

"You do taste good." He said smiling at me and then stealing another peck on the lips.

I blushed. When I was knocked out and he a had poured his heart out to me, he had said he wanted to kiss me when I still tasted like cherry. He got to and I liked it. Oh my gosh. I liked it. A LOT.

Chapter 16

I finished locking up the shop and led Trent out the back door back to Sal's house. My last time to work in the shop and my last night to spend here. It seemed surreal. At least I wasn't alone and I just had a mind-blowing, real first kiss in a place I loved. I smiled inwardly and said, "Sorry Sal."

We made it back to Sal's house and I got the key out from under the rock one more time and let us in.

"I've got to go hit the shower. I'm filthy after all that work. Would you mind ordering us a burger from the diner?" I asked Trent.

"Sure Dee baby. No problem, but don't take too long in the shower. I could use one too." He said winking at me.

I wasn't sure what the wink meant and I didn't dwell on it. I grabbed a tank top and some cotton shorts and headed to the shower. I got in and relived the kiss. It was so perfect. The way he held me felt so good. I wondered if I was wrong to let myself fall into the temptation. I was pulled out of my thoughts when the bathroom door opened.

"Dee baby, I was knocking. Could you not hear me?" Trent asked sounding worried.

"I'm sorry Trent. I'm ok. I was lost in my thoughts," I said.

"You were thinking about me huh?" He asked sounding cocky.

"What's it to you?" I asked playfully.

"Damn it baby. I'm sorry to barge in, but there's a Mr. Smith here to talk with you. He was Sal's attorney. He said he needs to go over the will with you. You must be pretty special for him to come to you instead of him call you in." Trent explained.

"Oh ok. Tell him, I'll be out soon. I only grabbed a tank and cotton shorts. Shoot. I didn't realize we would have company." I said.

"No worries Dee baby. I'll grab you something real quick," said Trent.

"Thank you. You rock." I hollered.

He just laughed.

I came out of the bathroom ten minutes later in blue jean capris and a pink polo shirt. Trent did well. He even grabbed me a nude bra. Luckily I already had panties in the bathroom. "Hi Mr. Smith. I didn't know you were coming by." I said going to sit across from him at the dining table.

"I tried calling the house number today, but no one answered." He said.

"Oh that's my fault. I ended up working in the garage today. Ms. Darla came by needing help and once I opened one bay door, the masses descended." I explained.

"I figured it was something like that. Sal always said you loved to work. I last saw him right after he turned 60. He got his will put together and it very much has everything to do with you," said Mr. Smith.

Mr. Smith looked over to where Trent was standing with question in his eyes.

"It's ok if he's in here. I trust him and he's with me." I said.

Trent came closer to me and laid his hand on my shoulder. "Sit down Trent. Let's see what Sal was up to." I told him.

"Ok well let's dive into this. I won't read all the law crap. It doesn't make sense anyways. But Sal was of sound mind when he came in, so there's no problems anyway. You my dear Dee Anne Rice are his sole beneficiary. He left everything to you, but with specific instructions for you and I. Here's his letter to you sweetheart. I know what it says already. I can read it out loud or you can take the time to just read it to yourself right now." Mr. Smith said holding a handwritten paper out towards me.

With shaky hands I grabbed it. "I'll just read it silently if that's ok."

Mr. Smith nodded softly.

*Dee girl,*

*If you're reading this that means I've kicked the bucket and I'm sorry. I had lots of plans for you. Oh and yes I wrote this by hand while Smithy watched. You know I don't do computers or whatever. I hope by now you know how much you mean to me. I love you Dee girl. You're my daughter to me and you're all I have, so naturally you get it all. There are few things you need to understand:*

*1) You will keep Betty until you die and drive her weekly. She loves to run. You're the only person besides me to ever drive her.*

*2) You get all the tools in the garage. Obviously I won't be needing them anymore, but you do. You're a damn fine mechanic.*

*3) Take whatever you want from the house and donate the rest to shelter. Tell them to come clean out the house and they will.*

*4) No. You don't need my house. It will be sold with the shop and garage.*

*5) Yes, it's being sold. Smithy has a buyer already. They know that Sally keeps her job and no I'm not selling it out from under you. Smithy will give you all the money that's made from its sell. It will be enough for you to start your own shop or go to college or whatever you want Dee girl. You deserve it all. And no, you don't need this shop. Make your own way. Get out of this town and away from the bad memories of Brian and get somewhere he can never hurt or steal from you again.*

*6) If you start a new garage on your own, make sure my picture is up on the wall somewhere. I'll be proud of you no matter what you do.*

*7) I sure hope I made it to your graduation, but just in case I didn't, I got you that Firebird you've eyed since you were 14. Fix her up, give her a good name, and paint her green.*

I had to stop and gasp. I let the tears fall. I had painted her green. I continued reading.

*8) Don't be afraid to be in a relationship with someone. You are not either of your parents. You are not them. You will do better. I don't want you to try to go through this world alone Dee girl.*

*9) Have some kids. You will be a good mother when you're ready. I've seen you with the kids that come in the store and how you light up giving them suckers. Of course not your cherry ones though. Again, let me say, you won't screw any children you have up. You are not your parents.*

*10) I know you remember the big, scary guy that you paid off for your dad when you were 13. His name is Tony. Find him. He's been looking out for you since the night you stumbled across him. I would like to take all the credit for keeping you safe, but I can't. Tony warned off any other goons from you if they were snooping around and he would give me a heads up if someone would be looking. So those random times I needed you to work or stay with me, it was to keep you safe because Tony said so. I don't know his last name. I never asked. He's not one to share much information with, but he's been on your side for a long time.*

*11) Don't be sad over me forever. Remember me. Smile when you think about me, but live life. You know I did and you were the biggest blessing of my life. Don't second guess yourself and listen to heart from time to time.*

*I hope I managed to write everything down you need to know. My hand is cramping up from all this. I love you so much Dee girl. You are a great mechanic, person, daughter. Now go make something of yourself and don't half ass it.*

*Sal*

The tears were falling freely now. Sal was still taking care of me. Trent put his arms around me and I clutched the note to my chest.

Mr. Smith spoke, "As you can see you get everything my dear. He loved you so much. Everything is already in order. You don't have to worry about a thing. The contract for the selling of everything is already done. I'll just need a bank account for the money to be direct deposited to. The sell with be complete in a couple months. You will be getting a large sum of money. I would suggest having something ready to invest in immediately following the sell. I can help you with that too if you need it. In the contract there is a contingency that Sally keeps her job. The shelter will be here in two days to clean the house out. Be sure to take whatever you want. And the beloved Betty is all yours. I'm sure you know where the keys are. If you need anything else or have any questions, just call me. My info is in this folder that I'm leaving with you. There's also a paper in there I need you to fill out for the bank deposit. I just need it in the next two weeks. The title to Betty is also in there. Now if I can get you to sign this document. This is just saying we are finished with this will and I you were told everything you need to know.

I signed the paper and shook his hand. I was still in shock. Mr. Smith let himself out. He and Sal had been friends. Mr. Smith always handed all the legal stuff for the shop. I looked at Trent wide eyed. He just hugged me.

"Sal took care of you Dee baby. You can have your very own garage anywhere. Everything will be ok." Trent said holding me.

"He gave me Betty. He loved that car. He said I was a good mechanic. I'm just so overwhelmed right now." I said breathing out.

"I can imagine. That was a lot to take in," said Trent.

"Could you do me two favors Trent?" I asked still feeling numb.

"Anything." He said with no hesitation.

I smiled. "Can you use your PI skills and find Tony for me? And will you for Pete's sake go pick up our burgers? I'm starving." I asked.

"I will do both of these. Keep in mind, I haven't showered yet, but I am hungry so I'll let that slide for one kiss. But for my PI services we will have to come up with some sort of payment plan. I'm thinking a make out session a day for the foreseeable future should cover all my fees." He said smiling devilishly.

I put my hand out to him to shake and said, "I accept these conditions. I'll start payment now." And I stood up on my toes and kissed him slow and sweet.

He smiled after I let my lips move from his and said, "I'll go get the burgers."

I watched him walk out the door and decided I'd take Sal's advice and listen to my heart and start living.

Chapter 17

The next day was the viewing and the funeral. I wore a knee length navy blue dress and black, closed toe heels. I wasn't ready for this day. But, I would never be ready for this. I grabbed Betty's keys and headed out to her. I had decided to drive Betty. Sal would have wanted her to see him off. Trent wore a nice black suit with a navy blue tie. I'm pretty sure Lilian color coordinated  us. I made it to the funeral home and parked Betty behind the sad looking hearse.

Mr. Baker met me right inside. He smiled warmly at me and grabbed my hand and squeezed it. I nodded at him. I had to do this for Sal. I walked into the funeral home room and saw the blue coffin with the stripes I had painted on it. I was scared to walk up and see Sal laying in there. Trent must have noticed my hesitation, because he grabbed my hand and laced our fingers together and squeezed.

I slowly walked towards the casket. I had to get this over with, because people would be coming soon. When I got there, he looked pretty good. He was in his coveralls, with his hair combed back, and his dirty, old cap in his hands on his stomach. I reached in and touched his cheek. It felt funny. This wasn't Sal, just his shell. I put a picture of him and I in his pocket and said, "Put in a good word for me would ya? I'm going to give this happiness thing a shot."

Trent's hand squeezed even tighter on mine when he heard that. I turned to look at him, my eyes full of emotion. I hoped he saw all that was in them. I was pretty sure he did, when he leaned down and pecked my lips. I walked over to the side of the room and took my place to greet people. There were a lot of flower arrangements. He had been the town's mechanic and gas station owner for thirty five years, so he touched a lot of lives.

Fifteen minutes before the actual funeral was to start, my heart swelled with emotion when I saw Trent's family walk in. All but Stephen and Haley were there, but his mom, dad, and sister were there. They walked up the aisle to me and hugged me tight. My eyes swam with tears.

"You're here?" I said wondering why.

"Dee we told you that you aren't alone. We are here to hold you up when you feel like you can't stand anymore. We are here to lend you our strength. We meant it when we said you are part of our family now," said Ma.

I hugged her again and whispered, "Thank you," in her ear.

Pop gave my shoulder a squeeze and I gave him a nod. Lilian hugged me again too and kissed my cheek. I looked to Trent with tenderness in my eyes. He read it. He hugged me tight and said, "There's no turning back now Dee baby. You are one of us."

Pop's lips curved into a smile. He knew I was letting Trent in. I looked over to the door and pulled away from Trent and all but ran up the aisle. He and the family watched as I rushed over to the big, scary man that just walked in. I recognized him immediately. He looked older, but he was still big and dominating.

"Tony?" I asked as I got to the man I knew from a dark day in my childhood.

He nodded and I jumped onto him. Luckily the big man caught me in his arms and held me tight. I don't know what had gotten into me. I guess all the hugging Trentolini's were rubbing off on me. He held me for a long while. I finally pulled away from the  huge man and looked right into his eyes. I told him, "Sal wrote a letter. I know what you did for me. Thank you. I know that's not adequate enough, but thank you. You're the reason nothing worse ever happened to me."

"No I'm not the only reason. Sal loved you and took care of you. I just told him things he needed to know sometimes and I knew after I met you that you were special and cut out for something more in this world than being a deadbeat's kid. You were brave and smart." Tony said.

"I owe you $276 and I intend on paying you back. I know you covered the rest for me. My dad had asked me where I got $1000.00 from one of the times he came back. I remember you said you had a daughter at home. I'll give you that money and you take her out for me." I said to Tony.

His eyes went misty. "I wish I could take her out Dee. She died from Leukemia when she was fifteen. That's one of the reasons I had to try to protect you. I couldn't do anything to protect her, but I could for you. I was scared I had failed when I heard you were with Trentolini's son. But when I came by the shop right after closing, I saw the way he kissed you. I saw the love. Maybe I didn't fail?" Tony said raising his eyebrows in question.

"Oh God. I'm sorry Tony. I didn't know. She was lucky to have a dad like you. I know you made her feel safe. And no, you didn't fail. Trent is special to me. He's been here for me throughout all this. It's been a crazy ride but we are in a good place." I told him.

His hard face went softer and he said, "Good."

"I still want to pay you back. I don't like owing anyone." I said to him.

He smiled at that, "You don't owe me anything. You never asked for me to help ya. Hey if you wanna pay me back, take me out to lunch one day and tell me all you've been up. Sal made me promise to show up for you if he couldn't."

"I would like that a lot. Come sit with me. You and Sal were closer than I knew. It would mean a lot to me." I said.

He followed me up the aisle. People stared as we walked by. It was a packed house. The whole town showed up for Sal. It made my heart swell with pride to see all the people who came to pay their respects. I went and sat down on the front row by Trent. Tony sat on the other side of me and Trent's family sat right behind me.

"Tony. I'm surprised to see you here and with our girl," said Giorgio.

"Dee's been my girl a lot longer Trentolini. We share some history and Ol' Sal here was a friend." He said a little harshly.

"You two know each other?" I asked.

"Yes we do. His employer and I go way back," Pop said.

"Oh makes sense. Tony has been my secret guardian angel. He means a lot to me now that I know everything. Tony, Pop has accepted me into his family. I will be doing some work on cars with him soon. I'm one blessed chick to have so many strong men to support and protect me now, " I said patting Tony's arm.

Tony loosened up some.

Trent leaned over and whispered in my ear, "Nicely done. But even though you didn't technically need my PI services seeing how Tony ended up showing on his own, I'm still expecting our make out sessions."

I put my forehead on his shoulder and laughed quietly. He kissed the top of my head. I felt Tony watching us. Tony eased even more as he watched us interact. He wanted to be sure that everything was ok. Then the town preacher walked up and the service began.

It was a very nice service. It took forty five minutes for everyone to walk by and say bye and pay their respects. When I finally walked out, I stopped dead in my tracks when I saw, non-other than my father leaning against Betty.

Chapter 18

"What's wrong?" Trent asked looking at me to see why I had just stopped dead still.

He followed my gaze to the car. "Is that Brian?" He asked.

I nodded. I wasn't sure what to do. I walked over to him slowly never taking my eyes off him.

"What are you doing here?" I asked.

"Well that's no way to greet your dad. I came to pay my respects to Sal. He was a good guy, " said Brian.

"He was the best," I said flatly.

Brian's eyes went wide. He saw the big, scary man headed our direction and then his gaze went to Giorgio. Trent made it to me first and wrapped an arm around my waist. He stuck his hand, "I'm Giorgio Trentolini Jr. I assume you're Brian."

My dad didn't take his hand. Instead he looked to me and down to Trent's hand at my hip. He asked, "Dee what is this? Are you in bed with men hunting for me? Did you help them find me?"

I laughed. "Seriously Brian? I just lost the only father I've ever known and I'm being cared for by a family and all you're worried about is yourself. Why should I be surprised? You don't have it in you to care about anyone but yourself. I could have been taken at any time because of your stupidity and gambling. It's a blessing Tony looked out for me. Trent has been here for me in the hardest time of my life. Here's the kicker Dad, you brought Trent to me. He was looking for you and found me instead. I guess I should say thank you for bringing this amazing man into my life who is nothing like you."

I was so angry. I let years of hurt leak from me. "Now, if you'll move, I need to get in my car and go bury my real father."

Brian looked at me dumbfounded. He didn't even look hurt. He looked mad. Then all he said was, "Sal gave you his car huh?"

My eyes went red. I was about to say something else when Tony grabbed Brian by the arm and said, "You've hurt this tough kid enough. You need to come with me now. You won't ruin the rest of this very hard day for her. You understand?"

Tony asked, but he wasn't asking, he was telling him as he drug him away from me. I noticed Pop follow. I looked up to Trent and he was looking at me with pride. Ma and Lilian came up and both hugged me together.

"You are such a strong girl. I'm proud of you for standing up for yourself and standing up for my son." Ma said.

Lilian said, "Ok Ma. We've got to let them go. The procession is ready to start. We have to go now. I need to get back to Haley, but we will have dinner again real soon. Call me if you need anything."

"I will thank you. And thank you all for coming. You being here, meant more to me than you'll ever know." I said looking into both their eyes.

We got into Betty and I revved the engine a few good times for Sal. We followed the hearse to the cemetery. I thought I would quit breathing when they started to cover him in dirt. But, Trent was right there to hold me and keep me steady.

We went back to Sal's and I packed the few things I wanted from his house. I took all the muscle car posters off my walls, the Jeff Gordon throw, and Sal's coffee mug. I also got all the framed pictures of us together and of him in front of the shop when he opened it. I grabbed my clothes that were there. I also was sure to grab my special pot plant that had kept my money safe for so long. Trent said he would send a moving crew that they used to come get all the tools out of the garage. I locked the door one last time and turned to walk to Betty.

Trent was standing outside of Tammy and I walked over to him and kissed him and told him, "Thank you for everything and for being here for me. I couldn't have made it through today without you."

He kissed me on the forehead and said, "Dee baby, we've made it past me knocking you out, you going through a medical crisis,  a family dinner, and now a funeral. I think we are in this for the long haul."

I smiled at him and got in Betty and headed back to the penthouse following Trent. I listened just to Betty run as we made our way back. She purred like a kitten. I thought of the day Sal let me drive her. I was so excited. Then, I thought about Brian. I wondered what Tony and Pop did with him. I smiled to myself. I called Giorgio Pop now. It didn't feel weird either.

We made it back to the penthouse and parked in the garage. I parked Betty next to Fiona. They looked good side by side and then Tammy was there too. "It's starting to look like a car museum in here." I said smiling looking at the sexy girls.

Trent returned my smile. "I like seeing them in here."

We got in the elevator to go up to the house. I took my shoes off. Trent was watching me smiling. Then, the next thing I knew. He had me up against the elevator wall kissing me. It took my breath away. He was such a good kisser. I tried not to think why he would be and just take the moment in. When the elevator dinged and the door open, he stopped kissing me.

"I'm so glad to be home. It's been a long couple days. I just want to put on your robe and sit on the couch." I said sighing in relief.

Trent was looking at me crazy. I wasn't sure why. Then, he marched over to me, picked me straight up in the air, and slammed his mouth on mine. He was kissing me so passionately. My heart was beating so fast when he let my mouth go.

"Not that I'm complaining, but what was that for?" I asked.

"You said you were glad to be home. You called my place home. That makes me so damn happy Dee baby," said Trent smiling.

I started smiling and said, "Yeah I did call this place home. I didn't even realize it."

He pecked my lips again and said, "Now go get comfy. I'll make us some sandwiches and meet you at the couch. I'll even let you decide what we watch."

So, I did just that. I put on cotton shorts and a little tank and wrapped up in his black robe. I just never gave it back after the first day. I loved his robe. He smiled when I walked into the living room. He had two ham and cheese sandwiches, potato chips, and a big cherry coke. I smiled back at him. He was only in a pair of basketball shorts. His chest was so nice. Seriously the guy was perfect. I went and took my spot by him. He tossed me the remote.

"Find us something good, " said Trent as he took a big bite out of his sandwich.

I flipped through channels and stopped it on a comedy. I could use a good laugh after such a long, hard day. But before I could let it go completely, I  had to ask, "Do you know what happened to Brian?"

Trent flinched a little at the question. "To be honest, I really don't know and I don't plan on asking. The only thing that's important to me is that he stays away from you and you don't get caught up in his bad choices," answered Trent.

I nodded and took a big bite of my sandwich and said, "Fair enough."

We both must have been starved. In less than ten minutes, we both had empty plates. Trent put his arm around me and I settled into his side. "This is nice," he said.

"MmHmm," is all I mustered out.

I was content. I was snuggled up to a hot guy, my belly was full, I had a car, I had clothes, my father wasn't going to hurt me again, and I was safe. I guess I was so content, I fell asleep. The next thing I knew it was morning and I was waking up squished into Trent on the couch. How we managed to both fit and sleep on that couch was something. Trent was holding me tight to him. I guess I was the little spoon. His arms were tight around me and I was holding onto his arms.

He felt me stir and said, "Good morning beautiful."

"Morning," I said.

He pecked my lips when I turned to look at the gorgeous man. "Gross, we have morning breath!" I shrieked.

"Aww Dee baby, a little morning breath isn't going to scare me." He said chuckling.

"Gross," I said again getting up to go to the bathroom and brush my teeth. I heard him still laughing under his breath as I walked off.

It was Sunday morning, so Trent was going to be home all day. After I brushed my teeth, I went into the kitchen to find he had started the coffee. He wasn't in there though, so I assumed he went to the bathroom. I rummaged around in the refrigerator and found bacon and eggs. Luckily, the pots and pans hung from a rack above the stove. I hadn't really explored his kitchen yet, but today I was going to. It was top of the line and I was excited.

First, I poured me a cup of coffee. I needed the glorious caffeine in my system. I cut the bacon in half and set it in a large pan. I had eaten enough with Trent to know he ate a lot. I found a plate and lined it with paper towels. I decided I'd just fry us some eggs in bacon grease after I finished the bacon and make some toast. It was a simple breakfast, but it would be good. I turned some rock music on in the living room on the TV and swayed in the kitchen as I cooked breakfast.

"I could get used to seeing this in the morning," said Trent smiling as he walked in.

I turned around from the stove real fast to see his smiling face. He closed the distance between us and put his arms around my waist. I looked up at him and kissed his chin and said, "Ok now back up while I cook breakfast. I need to pay attention. Oh and thank you for starting the coffee."

He kissed me real quick and said, "Of course Dee baby." And then he went and sat at a bar stool facing me work.

"How do you like your eggs cooked?" I asked.

"However you want to cook em," said Trent smiling at me.

I nodded. I'd cook his like I liked mine then. I noticed that I was happy cooking us breakfast. It felt normal to me. Then, I got a sinking feeling, there was still so much I didn't know about Trent and so much I didn't know that I wasn't sure if I wanted to. I looked at the man who had been so many things to me in such a short period of time and wondered what exactly he was to me now. I finished cooking breakfast and sat a plate in front of him and went around and sat in the other bar stool next to him.

I put my egg on my toast and cut through it with my fork. Perfection. It wasn't cooked all the way hard or runny, it was like jelly in the middle. I inwardly smiled. Having plenty of food was special to me. Trent cut into his egg too and took a bite.

"Dee baby this is the best egg I've ever eaten." He said.

I laughed, "I think you would say that no matter what. You're kind of a suck up after knocking me over the head." I teased.

"That's not funny. I mean it. It's really good. I've always either had them hard or runny," said Trent enjoying another bite.

We finished up breakfast and Trent went to put our dishes in the sink and started to wash the plates. I followed him in and started to clean my mess at the stove, when I asked, "Trent what exactly are we doing? What are we?"

He put his sponge down and turned the water off at the sink and turned to face me. "I think it's pretty clear that you're my girlfriend. Dee, you've never corrected me or anyone else when we call you my girl. I think you never corrected it, because it's really what you want. I hope I'm showing you that I want to be your support system. My family adores you and damn Dee, I do too. We crossed the just friends line a long time ago whether you want to believe it or not. And when you asked me to kiss you, Baby, there's no going back for me. As far as what we are doing, we are figuring it out together. Your new normal is about to be way more different than it already is after Sal's place sells. Now, that your dad, I mean Brian, is around and can held be accountable for his own debt, you owe my Pop nothing. If you want to leave you can, but that doesn't mean I'm not going to try to get you to stay. I need to know where this goes."

There he was again, being perfect and putting it all out there for me. I guess he knew putting myself out there was hard and he was always ready to take the leap for me. I studied him for a long time, trying to sort out everything that I was feeling and thinking.

"Trent, are you sure? I'm not exactly easy to be with. I don't know how to do this. I know I liked cooking you breakfast. It feels good and normal. I like when you hug me and it's not I have a lot of experience seeing how you're the only guy that's ever kissed me, but you're really good at that and I can't get enough and it makes me nervous. I'm nervous that I'm not good at any of this. Look at you, you are 26, got it all together, and freaking gorgeous. I'm not naïve. I know you haven't just been waiting for me to come along and it bothers me that anyone else ever touched you. And you are 26! I'm just 18. It's a pretty big age difference. I don't know Trent...This is a lot." I tried to explain what I was feeling the best way I could.

He nodded and then answered, "It is a lot. You may be 18, but you have been adult for a long time. You are wise way beyond your years and probably more mature than me in many ways. We connect on primal level and I know I need you. I understand your reservations about my uh, previous personal life. I've had my one night stands and even dated a couple girls, but none of them really meant anything. If I could I would take it back, but I can't. All I can do is promise, I won't push for anything with you that you're not ready for. I'll wait for you as long as I need to. As far as you not knowing how to do this, be a couple, be us; I don't either. I've never been serious with anyone, but I do have good examples in my parents and Lilian is married. I think we could figure it out together. For the record, you a freaking fantastic kisser."

I closed my eyes, letting his words hit me right in my gut. He was right. I have been making adult decisions for a long time. I felt our connection. If I was being honest, I felt it the first day in the shop. I trusted him I realized, even after everything. If I was honest with myself, it was hard pill to swallow that he held anyone else, but he said he's never been serious with anyone. I was so scared to be happy, because sooner or later the other shoe drops. I let Sal's letter hit my soul. "Live life," he had written. I opened my eyes.

All I said was, "Ok."

He raised his eyebrows, "Ok?"

I nodded, "Ok. Let's try. I'm going to live life and not be scared to be hap.."

I didn't get it all out, because Trent was to me in an instant picking me up off the ground swirling me around and crashing his lips to mine. He said, "I promise, I'll earn it Baby. I'll earn every bit of your trust and affection and I promise to give you the world."

Chapter 19

I woke up Monday morning to Trent trying to gently get his arm out from under me. We slept in his bed together. He didn't do anything, but hold me close. I had never slept so well, than when he held me close. I hadn't realized I hadn't slept well my whole life.

"I'm sorry. I was trying to not wake you," He said kissing my forehead.

"No, I want to at least drink a cup of coffee before you're off to work. Go get ready and I'll start the coffee." I told him.

He smiled really big and nodded and headed off to the bathroom. I stretched and went and started the coffee and then used the smaller bathroom. I looked in the mirror after rinsing my face off to wake me up and I smiled. I felt happy and domesticated. This was a feeling I wasn't sure I would ever get. I walked out of the bathroom and poured us both our coffee, his black, mine with a little sugar and half and half.

Trent walked out his room in a suit with a red tie. I raised my eyebrows up and whistled at him. He did look good. "Power tie?" I asked.

He smiled and nodded, "Yep. I'll be in a meeting today with some potential business partners with the hotel for Pop. He's trying to get me more involved with it and then I have a client to meet up with for a PI job."

"Sounds like an interesting day," I said handing him his coffee.

He nodded, smiled, grabbed his coffee, and kissed me. Not just a peck, but like a real kiss. I took a step back and looked at him smiling.

"For the coffee," He said smiling at me.

"Then, I'll be sure to make your coffee every morning, " I said not hiding my thoughts at all.

"Good. So what are your plans for today?" He asked me.

"Lilian texted me. We are going to go to lunch today and then she's taking me to see the boutique. I told her I'd only come if after we did grown up things, I got to see Haley." I told him.

Trent's smile got even bigger.

"What are you smiling so big for?" I asked him.

"You know it's not fair that you go see me niece while I'm working?" He asked mischievously.

"Oh it's not. You're just mad that she might like me more than you. I guess I should buy stuff while I'm out to make cookies, so the next time I see Haley, I can seal that deal." I said teasing.

"You ain't right Dee baby, but I love you." Trent said without thinking and then he looked at me wild eyed. He looked scared that he had done something wrong.

I guess my eyes were big too. I didn't say anything. I just took another drink of my coffee and pretended he didn't say he loved me. I wondered if he really meant it or it just kind of went along with what he was saying.

Then he grabbed my hand. He said, "I'm sorry Dee. I didn't mean to just blurt that out. It doesn't mean I didn't mean it. I just wanted to wait and the timing be perfect. Shit, Dee I'm sorry. I probably just scared the hell out of you. You don't have to say it back. Shit, I probably just made everything weird. Have fun today with my sister. I'll be back home around five thirty."

I looked into his eyes paralyzed for a moment by the words he just spoke. I leaned in and kissed his lips and said, "Ok."

He looked back at me and said, "Ok."

I walked him to the elevator and got up tip toes to kiss him before he left. "Have a good day Orgie." I told him smiling a little too big.

"You're killing me baby. I'll try to have a good day, but it'll be hard seeing how you're not going to be with me. Keep my sister in line." He said stepping into the elevator.

As the door closed, I felt a clinching in my heart. I didn't like seeing him leave. I was so used to watching Brian leave that it didn't bother me, but Trent leaving was hard. I almost expected him to not come back. I shook my head, he had just told me he loved me, even if on accident, he didn't take it back. I tried to process my own feelings. They wouldn't process. I went and made his bed and picked up a little. I started a load of laundry and sat at the bar drinking coffee and thinking. I was glad Lilian would be taking me for lunch. I needed to get out of my own head. My phone rang.

I answered it, "Hello."

"Dee it's Pop. Are you decent? I'm in the garage. I need to talk to ya." Giorgio said.

"I'm in a robe, but I'm covered up. I have hot coffee ready. Come on up," I said to him.

"Ok. Thanks," he said and hung up.

Two minutes later, the elevator dinged and Giorgio walked in and came into the kitchen. He walked straight over to the bar where I was sitting and sat down.

"You want some coffee?" I asked.

"Sure. Black please." He answered.

"Trent likes his black too. Guess he takes after you." I said pouring his coffee.

Pop smiled at that. I handed him his cup and noticed he saw the other cup on the counter by the sink. Giorgio was the type of man that didn't miss anything.

"You saw Giorgie off to work this morning?" He asked still looking at the empty cup.

"Yes. I made him coffee while he got ready. It's nice to visit for a minute over coffee before he leaves," I said.

Giorgio thought for a moment, "It's serious for him Dee. I think my boy loves you. Judging by the way you're making him coffee, I'd say the feelings are mutual."

That hit me straight in the heart. Did I love him?

Giorgio continued, "But I didn't stop by here to discuss my son's love life, although it is important to me that he finds a woman that makes him happy. I'm here to discuss Brian and our agreement about fixing cars. I need to know where you stand and what your plans are."

"Ok. Tell me what I need to know and I mean only what I need to know concerning Brian. If he's in the bottom of a lake wrapped in chains, I don't want to know." I said right to Pop.

Pop chuckled and said, "Dee darlin, I didn't off Brian. I know you're used to dealing with real shady characters because of him, but I am truly not one of those guys. I can see how your idea of me would be a skewed because of my bonehead son bringing you against your will at first. I did want to have a visit with you then to discuss getting my money back and figure out how you could help me do that. With that being said, Brian showing up yesterday and Tony grabbing him got that part taken care of. As it stands now, I own the house you lived in. Brian signed the house over to me, because he couldn't afford to pay me back."

I looked at him wide eyed. "So you at least get your money back and I don't have to deal with him again. That's good."

"Is it good Dee? Do you want me to keep the house? I will if you want to keep it. I know this thing with you and Giorgie is new and living with someone right of the bat is a little nuts if you ask me." He said.

I smiled at him and I decided my next words with my heart, but carefully, "Pop I don't care if you burn that house down. It was never a home. It served its purpose, but it holds only sad memories for me. I appreciate you asking me first. You didn't have to do that and it means a lot to me, especially since you owe me nothing. But that house means nothing. I don't care if I ever see it again honestly. Your son has given me a home, a place I feel safe and that means the world to me. But I'd have to agree it is nuts, but it's working."

Pop smiled at me. "I'm glad it's working. You two are good for each other. And don't say I don't owe you anything. You making my son happy will always have me indebted to you and plus you could have upset our whole family if you ousted his moment of insanity bringing you here like he did. You are a tough kid and I respect you. I'll just sell the house and get the money back then. I'd like to use whatever extra made on top of the twenty thousand that's owed to me to put down on making you a real mechanic shop."

My jaw dropped. "Seriously? You want to help me get my own thing started here?"

"Yes Dee darlin. My son wants you around and my family loves you. I always help my kids out." He said.

My heart leapt in my chest. He called me one of his kids. I smiled at him, "I think I would love that. Did Trent fill you in on what Sal did?" I asked

"He did. We will make sure Stephen helps you get all that lined out. There are some pretty steep taxes you could get if it isn't done correctly. That car of Sal's is gorgeous. So with what Sal left ya, you will have more than enough to start a real business. Plus you already have all the tools you'll need. The movers should be picking them up soon. Now, I would still like to buy some old cars for you to fix up for me. We do a charity ball every year at the casino and auction off real nice stuff. This year I'd like our main item to be a car. Are you up for that?" He asked.

I nodded ecstatically. "I'd love to. That sounds like fun. I've never been to a ball or anything for that matter."

"So I take it you want to start a shop here then?" He asked smiling.

I nodded real big.

"Good. Now my last bit to discuss with you, how do you know Tony?" He asked with his eyebrows raised high.

I told him the story of what happened when I was thirteen and how he spotted me the money I didn't have and I let him read Sal's letter to me.

Giorgio chuckled, "You definitely did a good job diffusing the tension between us. I wasn't sure why he was there. Tony is a tough guy and the guy he works for isn't near as nice as me. If you would have told Tony what Giorgie did, he would have probably took a baseball bat to him. I'm not saying not to be around Tony now. If he's taken care of you for so long, he has a soft spot for ya, but Tony is a hard guy. He knows bad men, but him being what he is, is probably the only reason you didn't have much worse happen to you growing up. See I do owe ya. Tony would have put a hurting on Giorgie if you'd asked him to."

My eyes were big. "I couldn't live with myself if I had someone hurt or worse. Tony and I will go to lunch one day soon. I owe him at least that much. I am lucky to have him in my corner, but I definitely won't be asking him what he's been doing at work," I said.

Pop chuckled again. "You're a smart girl. Ok I've got to get to the casino to go over some paperwork and get out of here so you can get ready for lunch with Lilian."

"You just know everything don't you?" I asked eyeing him.

"It's my job to know what my kids are up to. Now come over here and give Ol Pop a hug before I go." He said holding his arms out.

And I did. I hugged him tight and enjoyed the embrace.

"I don't know what your family is doing to me. I've never hugged or been hugged so much in my life," I said softly laughing.

"It's your family too now Dee and Ma and Lilian are both huggers. It tends to rub off on ya," said Pop and he headed for the elevator.

Chapter 20

Lilian was at the penthouse promptly at eleven to pick me up for our lunch date. She was taking me to her favorite place to eat and hang out. It was a little sandwich/bakery place. I was excited. I loved dessert. When Lilian saw me she cat called.

"Girl you look good in the hooker boots! If I had legs like you, I'd wear them every day!" Lilian screeched.

I smiled from ear to ear. It was nice to be complimented. I had on skinny jeans, a black blouse with bell sleeves, and my black leather boots I loved so much. I got in Lilian's SUV and we were off. I laughed out loud when I heard the music come through her car speakers. She was listening to a 90's boy band. I had never had girl time before and I was already enjoying this. We pulled into the sandwich/bakery shop twenty minutes later.

I ordered a chicken salad sandwich and a cup of vegetable soup. Lilian got a tuna sandwich and a cup of corn chowder. I took a bite of the soup and was in heaven. It was so good.

Lilian took a bite of her chowder and moaned. "God this is almost as good a sex," she giggled.

My face turned red and I didn't reply.

Lilian noticed and said, "Oh I'm sorry. I'm not trying to make you uncomfortable. I tend to joke about everything. I'm sure you don't want to talk about your sex life, seeing how your man is my big brother. But, seriously, this soup is almost as good as sex. I won't tell him if you agree. Just nod for yes." She was still giggling.

I stayed quiet again. I wasn't sure how to respond. Lilian was just trying to be funny and a friend. She studied me some more.

"Dee. I'm sorry. I know you don't know me very well. I promise no more sex talk. I didn't mean to make you so uncomfortable to where you won't talk to me," She said apologizing. Lilian felt bad.

I had to say something. I hated that she felt bad. It wasn't her fault. I decided to go with honesty.

"Lilian, it's not that I don't want to talk to you. I appreciate you trying to be funny and it really is funny, but it's only, well, I am uncomfortable talking about sex. It's not for the reason you think though, but it may be weird to talk about your brother to you. Anyway, the thing is, I can't talk about sex. I can't compare the soup, because I have nothing to compare it to," I said hoping she understood what I meant.

Her eyebrows drew together and then her eyes went wide. "Dee are you saying what I think you're saying?" She asked.

I nodded.

"You've never been with anyone?" She asked.

I shook my head no.

"Wow Dee. That's really something. I'm a little shocked to be honest. You're beautiful and smart. How has no guy snatched you up? I'm just surprised you live with my brother and he's not...ya know. Dee he must really care about you. A man doesn't just take care of a woman like he's doing with you if they don't really care about them," said Lilian.

I finally spoke, "He does care about me and I care about him too. The feelings are scary for me. I wasn't in a normal loving home or ever saw a normal relationship for that matter. I'm a little embarrassed of my life to be honest. Your brother was even my first kiss. I've never had a boyfriend or friends. I was basically raised by a bachelor, mechanic. My biological father left me to be on my own for the most part when I was ten. I had to figure out how to make it on my own. I was too embarrassed to have friends, because I couldn't ask them over and I was even more scared to do the boyfriend thing. The first new brand new clothes I received were from you the other day. I didn't even go to prom. I couldn't afford a dress. I never went to birthday parties as a child, because I couldn't afford a gift. Then, I quit getting invited to parties, because I never went. I had a lonely life."

I paused for a moment and then continued, "It wasn't completely lonely though. I had Sal and he took care of me. He taught me a skill so I could always find work. I never went without anything I needed to live. But I just lived. I didn't live. I'm trying to live now. I opened up and am giving this thing with your brother a real shot and I'd like to give us a real shot too. I've never had girlfriend around my age. It'll be nice. Please just be patient with me. I'm trying. I bet I sound pathetic."

Lilian got up with tears in her eyes and came around the table and hugged me. I hugged her back and told her, "Pop was right, you and Ma are huggers. I think you are turning me into one too."

She laughed and said, "We are. We all like you a lot Dee. My brother is lucky to have found a perfect flower like you. I'm sorry what you had to go through, but it made you the bad ass woman you are today. You are far from pathetic."

"Thank you," I said smiling at her.

She was right. All the bad stuff I lived through brought me to this point in my life. I had lost Sal, yes, but I had a whole family now and Trent said he loved me. Only one other person had ever told me that. Those words meant a lot to me. I knew if I said them, there would be no turning back for me, so I shocked myself when the next words ran from my mouth.

"He said he loved me this morning. I didn't say it back and he said I didn't have to. I've been thinking about it all day and I think it's because I've been trying to hide from my own feelings. Lilian, I love him. It scares me and I'm terrified that I don't know what I'm doing, but I love him."

Lilian smiled so big. "Well, I'm so happy I could burst. I knew he loved you and I was hoping you would return those feelings. You fit in with us so well. You're good for him. And you're good for Pop. No one actually knows what they are doing in new relationship. You just follow your heart and learn as you go. Don't just run away when things get tough. You have to work through things together. As far as the physical stuff goes, it's natural and you'll figure it out. If there's something you want to talk about, I'm here. Other than that, it won't matter if you know what you're doing. He loves you and that means something and makes making love mean something more too."

I smiled thinking about Trent. We had worked through a tougher time than Lilian knew about. We were solid. I told her, "Thank you for listening to me and being here for me. Everything you said makes me feel a million times better."

Lilian returned the smile and said, "Well that's what I'm here for! We are getting good practice in for when you're my sister!"

"Hey now! Don't jump the gun. Who says he's even going to ask me to marry him?" I laughed.

"So you're not opposed to it then?" She laughed.

"You're a mess!" I shrieked at Lilian.

"I know! Now let's finish eating so I can take you to see Haley," She said still chuckling.

We finished out lunch and went to the bakery part of the place. It was amazing and smelled of cookies and fresh bread. I picked Haley out an iced sugar cookie that looked like a lady bug and got two cherry turnovers for Trent and I for later. Lilian wouldn't let me get lunch, so I made her let me get dessert. She got a tripe chocolate brownie. I made her get Stephen something too and asked her what to get Ma and Pop. She told me Ma loves anything chocolate and Pop is a cannoli guy. I felt good buying something sweet for everyone. I had never had so many to people to care about and it was nice.

Lilian then drove us to Ma and Pop's house. Ma babysat Haley for Lilian while she worked. She said Ma wouldn't allow her to put her granddaughter in daycare or have a nanny. When we pulled in, Ma came out with Haley and they waved from the front steps. I got out carrying my bags of sweets and pulled the lady bug cookie out.

"Hey Haley girl! I brought you a prize," I said talking in my excited baby voice.

Haley's eyes went wide, "DEEEEEE!!! Cookieeee!" She screamed with joy.

I smiled so big my cheeks hurt. Seeing Haley get all excited made me so happy and she remembered my name. She came running to me and I immediately bent down to grab her. She took the cookie from my hand and bit it's cookie head off. I laughed.

"Tell Dee thank you," said Ma.

Haley just wrapped her little hand around my neck and kissed me on the cheek with her sticky little mouth.

"You're welcome Haley girl," I said kissing her little round cheek back.

She giggled and continued chomping the cookie.

I handed the bag to Ma and said, "I got you and Pop a prize too. Lilian told me what you liked."

Ma's eyes went soft. "Thank you honey. That was so sweet of you," she said.

We went inside and I played with Haley and visited with Ma and Lilian. Lilian told Ma that I had never even been to one of my proms, so that when it was getting closer to the charity ball, we were all going dress shopping together. I smiled and found myself really excited to go dress shopping with them. Haley loved me and I fell for that little girl. I let her lead me around and play with my hair.

"You're so good with Haley," said Ma.

"She's a precious little girl. I enjoy spending time with her. I've always loved kids," I said smiling.

"You will be a great mother one day when you are ready. I'm not saying that to sound like a baby hungry grandma. I really mean it as a compliment and I really believe that you will be a natural mother," said Ma looking sweetly at me.

"I hope so. Not too long ago I wasn't sure if I'd want kids, given how I grew up. But the more I go, the more I realize I'm way different than the people who gave me life. I wasn't sure if I'd ever be able to open up enough to let someone in either and then Trent literally put himself in my life and now I find myself opening up to more than just him," I said contently and nodding towards Lilian.

Lilian chimed in, "Ma I think I've got a new sister."

Ma said, "Oh yeah? I would love to have another daughter. He loves you doesn't he honey?"

I smiled and then answered, "He does and I realized today my feelings are the same. I love him too. I haven't even told him yet. I told his sister and his mom before I told him! Hope he won't be too upset that I had to admit to myself and you two first."

"I think he's just fine with it," said Lilian.

I looked at her confused. "What do you mean he's fine with it?"

Lilian nodded towards a doorway. I looked to where she nodded and Trent was leaned up against the doorway with his arms across his chest with the biggest smile on his face. I blushed and returned the smile, unspoken words being spoken in the look we gave each other.

At the same moment, Haley noticed her uncle. "ORGIEEE!" She hollered as she ran to him.

He swooped down and grabbed her up and hugged her tight and kissed her little cheek.

"I'm happy to see my girl. Did you have fun with Dee?" He asked.

"Deeee!!! Cookieeee!" She said and she wiggled down from his arms and ran to me and climbed in my lap.

I got up holding Haley and walked over to the doorway to him.

"So….I kinda love you Trent." I said looking at him.

He smiled, "I knew it!"

I slapped his arm and in turn Haley did too. I laughed. Trent bent his head down and planted a kiss right on my lips in front of his mom and sister and while I was holding Haley. I was a little stunned, but didn't mind. Haley wrapped a little arm around each of our necks and pulled us in to her and said, "Muah!"

Trent looked at me with such tenderness as I held Haley. I looked deep into his green eyes. Haley wiggled down to go back to playing on the floor. Trent closed in the distance between us and wrapped his arms around my waist. I wrapped my arms around him too. He smiled mischievously at me.

"So you love me huh?" He asked.

"So I do," I said.

"Good, because I was going to a breakdown if you didn't admit it soon. I love you so damn much Dee." He said pulling me close to him.

"Hey what's going on here?" Pop yelled from behind Trent.

Trent replied, "Nothing much Pop, just ironing out that Dee loves me."

"Oh yeah? That's good news. I assume Dee darlin knows you love her too then?" Pop questioned.

"She does indeed," said Trent looking at only me.

"Well, I'm glad all that's ironed out, now get outta my way so I can go kiss your mother," said Pop pushing his way through.

Ma stood up and welcomed Pop home with a smack on the lips. It was nice to see. He then bent down and picked up Haley and kissed her round cheek.

"What's that sticky red stuff on you shirt baby girl?" He asked Haley.

Lilian answered, "Dee bought her a cookie."

Pop looked to me smiling.

"Don't worry. I got you a cannoli. You didn't get left out," I said smiling at him.

"You're a good girl Dee darlin," said Pop nodding at me and then at Trent.

Trent and I didn't stay much longer. He was ready to get home, because he had another busy work day ahead of him. We said our goodbyes and I got my round of hugs from everyone. I left feeling full. When we got into Tammy, Trent nodded at the bag I was holding.

"I got us a couple cherry turnovers. I didn't forget about you either," I said winking at him.

Chapter 21

We rode home in mostly compatible silence. The air was heavy between us. So much had been shared that day. He held my hand the ride home. I smiled at our intertwined fingers and I looked up to him, to see he was watching me at a red light. I looked right into his green eyes and it hit me even harder in that moment; I love this man. A smile crept on his face. I think he knew what I was thinking.

When we pulled into the garage under the penthouse, I sighed in relief to be home. That warm feeling hit me again as I realized I was home.

Trent brought me out of my thoughts when he asked, "So I take it you had a good time with Lilian?"

"The best. She is really awesome. Talking to her helped me figure out my thoughts and feelings. She's so funny. I told her that her and Ma are turning me into a hugger. We talked a lot about you and me." I answered him.

He smiled. "You talked a lot about me huh? I bet she loved that."

"She did. She's happy for us. She loves you so much. Everyone in your family does. They are all looking out for you, ya know?" I asked him.

He nodded and said, "I know. I am very blessed in that department and now you are too. Dee they love you too and to see you with Haley. It just does something to me. When I heard you admit to loving me while holding my niece, I about lost it. You are one of a kind Dee baby."

I giggled, "Well I happen to like seeing you with Haley too. You're a great uncle."

We got out of the car and held hands walking to the elevator. He pushed the button and we rode up to the penthouse. I had my head laying on his shoulder and he kissed the top of my head and whispered, "I really do love you so much Dee baby."

I smiled into his shoulder and said, "And I really do love you so much too."

That's all it took him and he had me pinned up against the elevator wall, kissing me passionately. When the door dinged and the elevator opened, I realized that my legs were wrapped around Trent's waist and his hands were at my ass holding me up. I giggled. He carried me out of the elevator just like that too. I kept kissing him. He went to the living room and sat down on the couch with me straddling him. I felt vulnerable, but in a good way.

I had my hands wrapped around his face and I was still kissing him. He pulled back from me and said, "Whoa Dee baby. You better stop. This isn't how you want your first time. I want to make it special for you in every way. I love you too much to just let your first time be spur of the moment."

But in that moment, I grasped, this was perfect. Life isn't perfect in any way. I had just spent the day with his family, he loved me, and I loved him and all that mattered in that moment were the two of us. Plus the fact that he acknowledged wanting to make my first time special in every way, I finally had my answer; he was worthy of me.

I looked deep into his eyes and kissed him softly on the lips. I saw the hunger in his eyes and knew mine mirrored his. I kissed him once more. Then I spoke softly and directly to him, "Trent this is perfect to me. I love you and you love me and to be able to feel and acknowledge that is so precious to me. To know that you would move mountains to make something special for me, fills my heart in a way I didn't know it could be. This spur of the moment is perfect to me, because it's real."

Trent looked at me in awe. I could see the love, warmth, lust, and inspiration in his eyes. I wanted him and he wanted me. He stepped up from the couch still holding me and carefully made his way to his bedroom. I was trembling, but not from being scared. I was nervous, but I was trembling for the need to have him. I had never felt like I had to have anyone before.

"You're trembling Dee. You don't have to do this. I understand if you need time. I love you. I'll wait as long as you need me to," said Trent so full of love.

"Trent I want you. I'm trembling because I want you so badly. I'm nervous that I don't know what I'm doing, but I know having you now in this moment is what I need." I said confidently.

"Oh Dee baby." He said locking his lips on mine again.

He gently laid me down on his bed and kept kissing me. He stopped and slowly made his way down my body touching all the way. He got to my knees and grabbed my leg and unzipped my black, leather, knee high boots, and slid it off and threw it on the floor. He then, did the other and took off my socks and rubbed my feet. He worked his way back up to my mouth and kissed me again.

The kissing was hot and I mean hot. Trent worked his hand under my black shirt and grasped my breasts. I moaned and arched my back at his touch. He slowly pulled my shirt off me and lowered his head to my breast still restrained in my black bra and kissed the top of them before returning to my mouth. My body was heating up all over and tingling. The feelings I was getting overwhelmed my senses. I reached for Trent's shirt. I wanted his off too. He smiled on my mouth when he realized I was trying to undress him too.

Trent sat up and took his shirt off. My eyes roamed his broad chest and then his nice abs to the v I could see just on the top of his pants. He followed my gaze and smiled again. He reached down and pulled me up so he could unclasp my bra. I didn't even try to cover up as my bra slid off. I let him look. I wanted him to look. He slowly laid himself on me. When our bare chests touched, I felt a wonderful shock and loved the feel of his skin on mine. He continued to kiss me as his hands worked my breast and slid to the top of my pants.

Trent was taking his time. He unbuttoned my pants and slid the zipper down. He looked into my eyes before going any further. I nodded my head yes and he slowly put his hand in my pants and touched me on the outside of my panties. It felt good. I moaned at his touch. He kissed me again and was gently rubbing me. He sat up over me and put both hands in my waist band and pulled my skinny jeans and panties off. He sat at the foot of the bed and just took me in for a moment.

He slowly crawled back up my body, but stopped at my most intimate area. I about jumped out of my skin when he lowered his mouth to me and lapped me up. I arched my back and whimpered at the sensation that shot through me. Trent took his time devouring me and only after taking me to the edge did he truly, slowly, gently ready me with his hand. I pushed towards him when he filled me with his fingers. He was tenderly and thoroughly getting me ready. He was making it one hundred percent about me. He kissed his way back up to my mouth and then devoured my mouth while still working me with his fingers. I reached for his belt and started to unbuckle him.

Trent stood up and took his pants and boxers off in one motion and kicked his socks off. I took all of him in. I'd never seen a man naked before, but he looked like he could be a Greek statue. He was perfect. I licked my lips looking at him. He lowered himself back over me and was hovering. He looked deep into my eyes as if asking permission one more time.

I whispered, "Please."

He kissed me slowly and I felt his tip at my entrance and my heart hastened. I couldn't wait much longer. I pushed my hips up towards him. He took the hint and slowly entered me. He gave me just a little so I could adjust to being filled. It hurt a little, but it was ok. I really just wanted the rest of him. I pushed myself up onto him and took him myself. His eyes went wide in shock, but then he smiled at me and I picked my head up and kissed his chin.

Trent wrapped his arms around me and held me tight as he started moving slowly in me. I felt myself stretching to accommodate him. It hurt a little, but the sensation of being one with the man I loved outweighed any discomfort I had. I was completely connected to him in that moment. Instinct took over for me and I wrapped my legs around his hips to try to take more of him in. He moaned when I did that. I like to hear him moan, especially after all the moaning he had me doing. We kissed some more as he gently glided in and out.

Trent, then, took my hands and intertwined our fingers and held my hands above my head. He then lowered his mouth down to one of my nipples and swirled his tongue around it as he kept making love to me. I cried out in complete rapture and shortly after, Trent was groaning with his own release. He stopped moving and rested his forehead on mine. I smiled at him and he smiled back.

"I love you baby," said Trent.

"I love you too," I said taking in his face as he still was on top me.

I was in love with this man and there was no turning back for either of us. We made love and it shook both of our worlds to their core. I was hopelessly lost in this man.

Trent slowly rolled off of me and I immediately missed his weight on me. Then, he turned around and placed his arms under me and picked me up like a baby. He carried me to the bathroom and gently sat me down on the soft bath rug and started the shower. When he got it just right he held my hand and led me into the shower with him. We got in and he held me close to him. I had my back up against his hard chest and just let him hold me up. I was spent. My body ached but in a good way.

Trent gently washed me. I was a little taken aback at first, but then let myself enjoy the intimacy and the gentleness he showed me. I turned and faced him and held my arms around his neck and searched his face. I smiled at him and kissed his lips.

"What was that for?" he asked as the warm water sprayed us both.

"I love you and thank you for being so attentive to me. I really like what we just did," I said blushing.

"Good. I did too. Dee baby, that was…that was like a religious experience for me. It's never been that way for me. I was connected to you more than just physically. I never knew it could be that great. I didn't know I could feel so much. I love you too baby," said Trent as he kissed me again.

"I liked it more than I thought I would the first time. It did hurt a little, but then it felt so much…I don't know, more? Better? What you did to me…it was amazing." I breathed out as the water still washed over me.

He smiled really big. "I'm glad it was good for you. That's all I want, you to feel good and like it."

Trent finished washing me and I let my soapy hands glide over him and wash him in return. We got out and dried off and went to bed together. We never put any clothes back on. After having him, I didn't want any barriers in between us. I just needed to feel him. He held me close to his chest and I fell right asleep, safe in his arms.

Chapter 22

When Trent's alarm went off in the morning, neither of us wanted to get out of bed. I wanted to stay wrapped up in his arms forever with his naked body pressed against me. He squeezed me tight to him and I could feel his hardness pressing into my backside. I ground myself into him.

He laughed and said, "Dee baby. I have to get ready for work."

"I know." I pouted.

He reached his hands up and caressed my breasts.

"I thought you had to get ready for work," I said breathily.

"I do, but you make me not want to," He whined.

Trent kissed the back of my head and slid his arms loose and went to the bathroom. I was sad to see him go. I got up and put his robe on and went to the other bathroom. I was sore between my thighs. I stepped lightly and thought it may be good that Trent didn't take me up on my silent offer earlier in bed. I then, got our coffee ready and heated up the cherry turnovers. I figured it would be ok to have them for breakfast.

Trent came out in black pants and a white button up shirt. It was PI day for him. I smiled up from my cup of coffee at him. I had his coffee and both turnovers on a plate in between the two bar stools that we sat in for our morning coffee. He smiled at me and came and took his seat.

I picked up one of the turnovers and took a bite and moaned as the cherry hit my tongue. Trent was watching me with a steamy look on his face and he leaned towards me. I got ready to kiss him, but instead he took a giant bite of my turnover!

"Hey boy! Back up! I got you your own!" I teased.

"But yours tastes better," he said winking at me.

I laughed and took another bite. We drank our coffee and finished the turnovers off happily. I walked him to the elevator and kissed him before he got in to leave.

"I'll see you when I get home baby. I love you," Trent said stepping into the elevator.

"I love you too," I said back smiling at him as the doors closed.

I sighed happily and made my way back to the kitchen to wash the coffee cups and plate we'd dirtied. I wasn't sure what to do with myself. I had no plans for the day. I decided to call Tony. I owed him a lunch and I just wanted to visit with someone who somewhat knew what I came from and get some advice. I picked up my phone and dialed him.

"Dee! Is everything ok?" Tony questioned instead of just saying hello.

"Well hello to you too. Everything is more than ok. I was just calling to see if you had plans for lunch today," I said smiling into the phone.

"Actually I'll be free at 12:30. We could do a late lunch. Meet me at Mario's Italian Place on Main at 12:45," Tony said.

"That sounds great. I'll see you there. I'm looking forward to visiting with you. I'm still getting settled in here and it's nice to have someone I trust close by," I said.

"I'm very happy you called. I can never turn lunch down with a pretty girl. See you then Dee," Tony said and then hung up.

I lazed around the penthouse, until it was closer to time. I got ready and put my hair in a messy bun, put on some old blue jeans, a Metallica t-shirt, and my black converse shoes. I was going comfy. I decided to drive Fiona. I got in and put on the aviator sunglasses Trent gave me and some clear lip gloss and headed out.

Thank goodness for Google maps. I made it to the restaurant in no time. I parked and a young man was watching me from across the parking lot.

"Wheeeww. That is one fine car!" He hollered from across the parking lot.

"Thanks! She was worth all the work!" I hollered back and kept walking.

He moved and started to follow me.

"My name is Sam. What's yours pretty lady?" He asked smiling at me.

I tried to smile and said, "Dee."

He kept step with me.

"I really like your car. Who did you get to restore it? They did a good job," said Sam.

"Thanks and me. I did all the work on her." I said now side glancing at the guy.

"What? You did that? Wow. I'm impressed." He said.

"You're surprised a chick knows her cars?" I asked.

"I didn't mean any offense. Not many women do the whole car thing. I'd sure like to get your number and go have a drink sometime." Sam said trying to play it smooth.

"That's a sweet offer, but I'm not on the market. I'm in a relationship already," I said turning getting a little nervous.

"Baby, what he doesn't not won't hurt him. I won't tell if you don't," Sam said, seeming more sleazy to me with every moment that passed.

"I'm not that type of girl. No thanks…" I didn't finish getting the rest of my sentence out when a big, deep voice sounded from behind.

"She's not old enough to get a drink with you anyway and she's clearly said no thank you. It's time for you to move along son, or I'll move you myself." It was Tony and he was clearly not amused by the sleaze ball Sam.

"Whoa man. I'm sorry I didn't mean to upset anyone. She's a pretty girl. You can't blame a guy for trying. Baby why didn't you tell me your dad was behind us?" Sam asked starting to look nervous himself.

"Whether he was behind us or not, you should've have dropped it when I said I was in a relationship Sam. I appreciate your liking my car and thinking I'm pretty, but it doesn't sit well with me when someone doesn't understand the concept of no. Now if you'll excuse me, I need to eat some lunch with my…"I looked to Tony. I wasn't sure what to call him.

He answered for me, "Father that's here."

Sam hurried off in the other direction as soon as Tony took an invading step forward and towered over Sam and scowled down at him. Tony gave him the stink eye all the way to his car. I gave Tony a weird side hug and said, "Thank you for scaring that jerk off."

"I'll always do my best to protect you, but I'm sure you could've handled yourself with that little guy," said Tony.

I laughed. Tony called a guy that was six foot tall a little guy. He held the door open for me and the delicious smell hit me. It smelled of oven fire pizza. My mouth watered.

"This place has the best pizza," Tony said leading me to a table in a corner, "And this is my table."

I laughed. "You have your own table here?"

"Well yes. They have the best pizza. I come in a couple times a week," he answered.

I smiled at this and sat down.

"So how are things going with you? With Giorgio's boy?" Tony asked.

"Things with Trent are really good. He takes good care of me and I love his family. They are good to me too. That's kinda what I want to talk to you about…Giorgio..Is he a bad guy? I mean he's really good to me, but you know how Brian was and I just don't want mixed up in anything like that." I said looking down.

"I see," Tony said. He continued, "Giorgio is one of the good guys when it comes to certain kinds of people. I have a great deal of respect for him and many times wished I worked for him instead of my employer, but don't you go repeatin that. I was concerned that Giorgio was just after getting the money back Brian owed him and that you got caught in the crossfire. I never wanted you to have to pay for Brian's bad judgement, especially after the encounter I had with you when you were barely thirteen. A daughter shouldn't have to do that."

I smiled longingly at him. "You're right a daughter shouldn't have to do that. I met Trent before I met Giorgio. He's a dominating guy, but a real family man. He loves his son and daughter and his wife too. It's nice to see. Thanks again for stepping up for me when I was a kid and just now outside. You said you were my father and I have to say I don't hate the idea of that seeing how I don't have anyone now that Sal's gone," I said smiling warmly at the big, scary guy.

Tony's face went soft at that. "I don't hate the idea of it either Dee. I missed out on getting to raise my daughter into adulthood and to see you doing well means a lot to me."

"You're one of a kind Tony. I've never met a harder soft guy than you. I will never ask you about your work, I know you can't talk of it and I don't really want to know what all you have to do…But promise me that I'll never have to worry about someone coming after you or me, because I care about you," I said looking into his deep, dark eyes.

He nodded. "You have my word you will always be safe, but as for someone coming after me…Well, some people get their feelings hurt when I do my job. I'll be safe though. I've learned certain skills throughout my years. I will be fine."

"Tony are you still married?" I asked.

He shook his head no. "Nope. Some marriages just can't make it through losing a child and mine was one of those. I was a reminder of what she lost every day and she couldn't handle it. I would have stayed with her no matter what and I still love her. I love deeply kid, but I let her go so she could try to find happiness again. She's remarried with a kid now. I'm happy for her. And seeing how I travel with my job and it's certain inconveniences, I didn't think remarrying would be smart. It's hard for someone to know kinda what you do for a living and think you can be loving and caring. I may be a big tough guy capable of many things, but I'm still human."

"I'm sorry Tony. Anyone would be lucky to have your love and safety. I know I'm lucky to have you. I wish I would have known sooner. We could have been doing lunch together before now," I said smiling at him.

"Dee, I didn't know what you would think after I scared you that night. I didn't want you to think I was some creepy, old man stalking you. You had enough worries. You didn't need to worry about me too. I know what I look like. That's one of the reasons I'm good at my job. Being intimidating is a good thing for me, but not for when I want to help a young kid," Tony said.

"Intimidating on the outside, marshmallow on the inside," I laughed out.

"Hey don't ruin my reputation!" He squawked at me.

The pizza came and he was right. It was the best pizza I'd ever eaten. We ate a large pizza together and laughed and enjoyed each other's company. I'd never dreamed that I would be sitting across from Tony casually eating lunch. He was the guy my nightmares were made of as a kid and now I knew he was the one actually keeping the nightmares away from me.

We finished eating and I had one more thing to ask, "Tony where do you bank at? I need to start a bank account and honestly, I don't know where to begin. Sal left me everything for the most part and I have to send my bank information to his attorney, but I have no bank."

Tony smiled at me. "Kid, I can help you with that. I use a credit union nearby. They are very quiet about their goings on and clients and the interests rates are top notch. Follow me and I'll take you over there and introduce you to my banker. They'll set you all up."

I did follow Tony and he introduced me to who I needed and helped me set everything up. I could tell he enjoyed this milestone with me. He was doing something with me he never got to do with his daughter. He was giving me advice and explaining how he put his money away and how to invest. His eyes lit when I'd ask a question and when I caught on to how to do things. His banker sent everything over to Sal's attorney and now all I had to do was wait for the money to be transferred when everything was sold.

I hugged Tony in the bank parking lot and told him thank you for all the help.

He said, "Anytime kid. I enjoyed this. I don't get to do stuff like this ever. I'm more than muscle. I do have a brain up top. If you need help with anything or anyone bothers you, you let me know."

I smiled and said, "Sure thing T-Daddy. Thanks again."

He smiled so big and for a moment my big, scary guy looked anything but scary. But, he ruined the moment and said, "Tell Trent or whatever if he breaks your heart, I'll break his legs. And I mean it."

I laughed and nodded and we went our separate ways.

Chapter 23

I stopped by the grocery store on my way back to the penthouse. I wanted to cook something nice for Trent. I picked up two quail, some asparagus, potatoes, and garlic bread. I would bake the quail and sauté' the asparagus and make butter, garlic potatoes. I also picked up stuff to make a cheese cake and of course got cherry pie filling to go on top. I smiled all the way home, excited to cook for the man I love.

When I got home, I got up to the kitchen, turned on some Nirvana, and got to work. I danced and sang as I got the cheesecake together. They were a pain to make and took a long time to bake. I put it in a water bath and set the timer. As soon as I pulled it out, I'd need to get the birds in the oven or dinner wouldn't be ready on time. I got my garlic minced and potatoes cut and asparagus ready for the pan. I felt in my element cooking. I was good working with my hands whether it be on a car or a meal.

As soon as the timer went off on the cheesecake, I pulled it out and notices it had cracked some on top. I was disappointed, but decided not to sweat it. I'd cover the crack up with cherry pie filling. I set the cheesecake aside to cool completely and threw my seasoned quail in the oven. I let them bake for a good while before starting on the sides. I wanted everything to be hot when Trent got home.

The timing was perfect. As Trent came though the elevator, I was getting the plates ready for us. He smiled when he saw me fixing his plate.

"Oh Dee baby, that smells fantastic. I didn't realize you were going to be making me a five star meal," Trent said coming closer to kiss me.

I replied, "I actually love to cook and I wanted to cook for you. I hope you like quail."

"Love it and love you. Let me go to the bathroom and wash my hands and I'll be right here to devour every bit of you, I mean the food," he said playing with me.

I giggled and finished up. I took our plates to the table instead of eating at the bar like we did so often. I wanted to sit down at the table tonight and act domestic. He came right back in and sat down at his plate.

"Baby, you really outdid yourself," he said.

"Well you can't say that until you try it," I said back smiling, because I knew it was good.

He took a big bite and groaned with delight. He ate every bit of food on his plate and his eyes went wide when he saw me come from the refrigerator with a homemade cheesecake.

"You made dessert too?" He asked smiling.

I nodded at him, cutting him a piece.

"Dee baby, I want to lick the cheesecake off of you," Trent said with his voice getting heavy.

"Ok," I said, "Off of where?"

His eyes smoldered and he licked his lips and said, "You just bring me that piece and I'll put it where I want it."

I did as he said and set the dessert plate in front of him. He swiped his finger through it and licked it.

"MMmmm. That's real good baby and it's going to taste better on you," Trent said pulling me to him.

He put his hands under the bottom of my shirt and rubbed up to cup my breasts. Then, he grabbed the bottom of my shirt and stood up as he lifted it from me and then he unclasped my bra and threw it to the floor. I smiled up at him in anticipation. He swiped his finger through the cheese cake again and covered my nipple. I got goose bumps from the chill of the cheesecake.

"Mmm. Yes. That looks so good," he said as he lowered his mouth to my nipple taking it all in and sucking hard and then swirling his tongue around in circles on it.

I let out an airy moan and clutched his head to me. His hot breath taking the chill from my nipple. I felt the sensation to my core. He did the other the same way and any soreness I had from the night before disappeared as my need for him grew. He then took his cheesecake covered finger and put it in my mouth. I sucked it clean and lapped at his finger with my tongue. His eyes grew even more heated. I knew what I wanted then.

I unbuttoned his pants and pushed them down along with his briefs to the floor. He looked down at me smiling. I grabbed him. It was a little awkward for me because I had never grabbed a man before, but I slowly stroked him, enjoying how smooth he was. He hissed through his teeth at my touch. I liked what me just touching him did to him. I looked him in the eyes as I swiped my finger through the cheesecake and rubbed it along the length of him. He watched me so intensely as I bent to my knees and ran my tongue along him where I had painted the cheesecake on him. He let out a heavy breath when my tongue reached his tip.

I smiled to myself. I honestly had no clue what I was doing, but he seemed to like it so I kept going. I kept licking and tasting him. He tasted good mixed with the cherry from the cheesecake. Finally, I put my mouth around his tip and slowly glided my way down the length of him as far as I could go. He moaned and arched. He liked that, so I did it again and again. I thought about how he touched every inch of me the night before and how much I had liked it, so I did the same. I rubbed my hands starting from his knees up to his groin. I slid them towards where my mouth was working and touched every inch of him. I reached and rolled his balls in my hand and he let out another moan. Good. I was doing ok for not having a clue. I rubbed his thighs and then used one hand to help with my efforts and the other to cup him.

Trent stopped me and pulled me to my feet. I looked at him confused.

"Baby, I love what you were doing just then, but I don't want to finish like that and if I didn't stop you, I wouldn't be able to hold on much longer. I want to be inside you." He breathed out.

I felt like I was going to turn into mush at his words. He let his hands trail over my chest to the top of my blue jeans. He unbuttoned them and pushed them down.

"Damn baby, you are perfect," he said taking in my naked body.

"So are you," I breathed out as he took my mouth in his.

Trent pushed me up on the table as he slide the cheese cake plate over. He stood in between my open legs and kissed me pushing himself against me. He stepped closer into me and I could feel him throb with each touch. Trent slid his finger down to my heat and rubbed to ready me.

"Baby you're hot for me. Are you ready for me?" He asked kissing behind my ear.

"Trent, yes, please." I begged him.

He positioned himself and thrust in in one motion. It took my breath away. It hurt but in a delicious way. I wanted more. He was moving at a steady pace, but it wasn't enough. I needed more.

"Trent, please. Faster." I moaned in his ear and then bit it.

He got the hint and pounded into me, my body and the table jolting with each thrust. I wrapped my legs around his waist and rode it out. It was amazing. His thrusts became more rapid and he was getting close. He gritted his teeth holding out for me. When he placed his thumb over my love button, I came undone and he did too. We both cried out together.

Trent rested his head on my shoulder as I still had my legs wrapped around him and my arms around his neck. "Trent that was..was..everything." I said.

"It was. Thank you for the cheesecake. It really was the best one I've ever had," he said smiling.

"It was the best one I've ever tasted too," I replied giggling.

Chapter 24

Trent and I were in bed later after showering and actually eating a piece of cheesecake, when I told him, "Oh Tony told me to tell you that he'll break your legs if you break my heart. I just wanted to throw that out there and warn ya."

I felt Trent's body shaking with laughter. He said, "It's only funny because he really means it. Leave it to me to fall in love with a woman who has a hitman looking after her."

"No. He wouldn't really hurt you!" I said firmly.

"Baby, if I hurt you, he would most definitely hurt me. He adores you. Good thing I plan on keeping you here with me forever. Dee baby you make me so happy and that meal you cooked me was fantastic." Trent said to me squeezing me tight.

"I'm so glad you liked it. I really do love to cook. You keep me around and I'll keep cooking for you," I said squeezing his arm.

"Pop will be here in the morning to get you. He wants to take you to see the warehouse he has that you can use to work on the old muscle car for the charity ball," said Trent.

"Sounds good," I said and fell fast asleep.

The next morning went the same; coffee, quick breakfast, and a kiss in front of the elevator to see Trent off. Pop was at the house at nine to take me to the warehouse and go over my work space.

Pop drove me to the warehouse in his Rolls-Royce . We made small talk along the way. I told him about the new bank account and that Sal's place would be officially sold in few weeks. He listened intently and gave advice where I needed it. He was a smart business man so I took his advice to heart.

When we pulled off a main road into a giant warehouse, I was shocked. It was in one of the busiest parts of the city. I followed Pop out of the car. He pushed in a key code on a pad by a door and he opened it up. I took in a deep breath when I saw what was in there.

There were four car lifts in there and all my tools and Sal's tools were set up neatly in there in toolboxes and work benches and tables. There was also really great lighting and my old muscle car posters were framed and hung in a row on one of the main walls. It took my breath away and mist hit my eyes. I let the tears fall when I saw a bouquet on my tool box from Sal's. It was a small bouquet of nothing but cherry Tootsie Pops tied with a green ribbon. There was a note attached to it. I picked it up.

*Baby,*

 I could see the thought that went in to putting the garage together. I walked past the posters on the wall smiling and then my heart broke and healed all at once when I saw the framed picture of Sal in front of his place. There were also four old muscle cars begging to be brought back to life. I took in a sharp breath and headed towards them. The first one was a 1970 Plymouth Barracuda. The second was a 1970 Chevy Chevelle SS. The third was a 1969 Pontiac GTO judge and the last was a 1968 Dodge Dart 426 Hemi. I couldn't believe there was a 1968 Dodge Dart 426 Hemi in my garage. I went straight for the Dodge Dart. Pop's eyes followed me as I walked around her, running my hands on her and looking down at her body.

"You are beautiful." I breathed out to the car.

"Trent said you would like that one," said Pop.

"He knows me well. You know only 80 were released and were exclusively created for drag racing. It could reach a quarter mile in ten seconds! That meant it was one of the fastest factory vehicles of its time. I can't believe I'm touching one in my garage. What you and Trent did for me...I have no words. Thank you so much," I said wrapping my arms tightly around Pop.

He chuckled, "I should of known you would give me a history of the car. You are more than welcome Dee darlin. This is a smart investment and you have work to do. You have six months to get one of these babies perfect for auction," said Pop hugging me back.

"Which one do you want for the auction?" I asked hoping he wouldn't say the Dart.

"Well, the Dart is Trent's. Trent insisted that it be for him and you. You know he loves his Dodges. Which one do you think would go over best for the auction?" He asked.

"I think the Chevy Chevelle. It is an SS 454 and it  would bring in the bucks. It's an iconic car and even people that don't enjoy muscle cars know that one. We could paint her candy apple red with black stripes and her top comes off, so she's sexy. Not to mention she has 450 horses under that hood," I said answering his question.

"That sounds good to me. Fix her up how you see fit. You are our car guru. Fix the other two up too and we will sell them for a pretty penny," Pop said nodding.

"Ok I'll keep up with how much goes into them so you make sure you get your money back and then some." I said.

"Dee, hire someone to do your books. You will have more than enough startup capital to hire several people. And you will be getting paid for your work, even if it's for me. You just worry about doing your magic and taking care of customers," said Pop.

I nodded. I still couldn't believe I had my own shop.

"Ok Dee. I have a busy day ahead me. You stay here and set the garage up how you like and get started on those cars. Trent will swing by to pick you up later. One more thing before I go." Pop said raising his eyebrows.

I looked to him with my head tilted to the side awaiting his command.

"What are the cherry suckers for?" He asked.

I laughed. "Cherry is my favorite flavor and I like to pop one in my mouth as I work and especially think on tough jobs.

He nodded and headed off.

I turned and looked at my garage again. She needed a name. I walked back over to the Dart. She looked brand new. She didn't need any work. She must have cost a fortune. I would have to ask Trent about it later. I went over to Sal's picture on the wall. "Well Sal, I've got a garage. I'm going to do this and do it well. How about Goon's Garage? Thank you for still taking care of me." I whispered to his picture.

I could almost hear him in my head telling, "Dee girl don't half ass it and do your best. You were taught by the best." Of course the best being him. I smiled.

When Trent walked in, I was on a roll cart under the Chevelle.

"Dee baby! It's me. I'm here," said Trent shutting the door behind him.

"I'm under the Chevy. I'm checking a few things. I'm almost done for now," I hollered from under the car.

I heard his footsteps getting closer. I smiled. I knew what he was here for, besides picking me up. He took his foot and put it on my cart and rolled me out from under the car.

"Dee I said I was here. I'm pretty sure your text said as soon as I got here, you wanted me to bend you over the dart and take you," said Trent smiling mischievously.

I had sent him a long mushy text, thanking him for everything and that I loved him so much and couldn't believe all the thought he put into the place. I may have also said I wanted him to bend me over the dart and take me from behind and then take me on the hood of the Barracuda the next day and then so on until we had christened every car. I blushed and smiled back at him.

"Did you lock the door Trent?" I asked him getting up off the cart.

"You know I did. I am already rock hard. I had a semi all day thinking about bending you over our new baby," said Trent starting to fumble with his belt.

I smiled and took my shirt off, looking at Trent. The room was getting hot and the air heavy. I then turned away from him and slowly took my pants and panties off. I bent over as I pulled them down so he would get the full view. I heard him groan. I walked over to the Dart and waited for him. He walked slowly up behind me and wrapped his arms around my waist and worked his hands up to my breasts, giving them attention, and then to my face. He pulled my head back and around to meet his mouth. He kissed me like he was starving. I loved it.

He kept kissing me as he worked one of his hands back down to in between my thighs. He then took his legs and parted mine and bent me forward over the rear of the Dart. He entered me hard and we both cried out in total bliss. He took me hard. I lifted one of my legs up to rest my foot on the bumper so he could get better access.

"Oh Dee. Yeah just like that. I like that. You're so hot on this fast car," he was panting in my ear.

It was totally working for me. We weren't making love. He was taking me greedily and I freaking loved it. I loved the feel of the cool metal of the car under me and Trent's heat behind me. This was a freaking hot moment and I would never forget it. He had his hand in between my legs working me and he was pounding fast and furious.

"Trent. I'm going to.."

He cut me off, "Wait for me. Wait."

"I don't think I can," I breathed out.

"Baby wait for me." He said struggling.

"Trent. I need to." I cried out.

"Now baby. Now. Together." Trent said pumping even faster.

We both cried out and were completely racked. We both slumped over. I hadn't experienced it like that before and I totally loved it.

"Trent you're amazing." I said breathing heavily.

He laughed with his head on my back and said, "Baby you're the amazing one."

Chapter 25

My days now had a routine to them. I saw Trent off to work and then would drive either Betty or Fiona to Goon's Garage and work on my new projects. I had plenty to keep me busy. Sal's attorney got everything finalized and I had $427,645 transferred into my account. I started up an LLC and Pop's attorney helped me get all the paperwork in order. I spent my days finding vendors for oil and parts and under hoods. I was loving life. Trent would stop by when he was done and we christened everything from the cars to tool benches and my desk. Life was good.

Lilian stopped by one evening after closing to find an eye full. I was riding Trent while he sat in my chair in my office. We didn't hear her come in. Family had the key code to get in. I had my office door shut and the blinds closed, so we didn't see or hear her come in, nor did I hear the text she sent.

She opened the door of the office to see her brother naked in a chair, taking a cherry sucker from my mouth and putting it in his and me bouncing up and down on him with my boobs flying in his face.

"Oh shit! I'm sorry! Shit!" Lilian screamed as our eyes locked.

I stopped dead still in horror.

She slammed the door back shut.

Trent started to laugh with the sucker still in his mouth.

"Oh my gosh Trent! This isn't funny! Your sister literally got an eye full. Oh my gosh. What am I supposed to say now?" I rambled totally freaked out.

"You say nothing. We are two adults that love each other. She'll probably be happy for us. She has a kid. It's not like she doesn't know how things work. It's fine," said Trent holding my face in his hands.

"Ok. I better get dressed and see what she stopped by for," I said with my face still beet red.

"We will finish this at home Baby," Trent said swatting my butt.

I opened the door to find a giggling Lilian.

"Umm. Hey Lilian." I said not meeting her eyes.

Trent walked behind me and wrapped an arm around me.

"Hey you two crazy kids. Good for you two," said Lilian still giggling.

"You and your brother are something else. He laughed and your giggling and I'm over here ready to die." I said looking back and forth between the two.

"Oh Dee. Who cares? It was just me. I'm seriously happy for the both of ya. You should be enjoying each other. It's my fault. I shouldn't of just dropped in. You didn't reply to my text and I should've of known better than to just stop by on two people madly in love." Lilian said.

I sighed. "You aren't going to hold this over me forever now are you?" I asked her.

"Of course! That's what sisters do. So like when we go shopping and I see a good office chair, I may air hump it or ask you something like, hmm that one looks wide enough for two doesn't it?" She said laughing.

I shook my head and felt Trent tremor with laughter. "Whatever. So what brings you by Lilian?" I asked.

"Two things; Ma wants us over for dinner in like an hour and I wanted to get you to work on Stephen's Porsche for him as an anniversary gift from me. I want it to be a surprise. I'm going to tell him you can't work it in until after the charity ball."

"When's your anniversary?" I asked.

"In a month," Lilian said.

"That doesn't give me much time, but I'm sure I can manage it for family," I said smiling at her.

"So Ma wants us over for dinner tonight?" Trent asked.

"Yep. She just told me today too. I'm not sure what for, but we should head that way." Lilian said shrugging.

"Great. You walk in on us in the middle of…and now I'm going to Ma and Pop's smelling like gas and sex." I said internally freaking out.

Trent let out a bellow of a laugh now. I looked at him irritated and it didn't help that Lilian joined in on his laughter. I couldn't help it either. I started to laugh.

Lilian left shortly after our encounter. I went back in the office to tidy it back up. Trent came up behind me as I was bending over to pick up some papers that had gotten thrown down. He wrapped his arms around me.

"Dee baby, it's really ok. She won't say anything to Ma and Pop. And you won't smell like sex by the time we get there, just gas," Trent said still quaking with suppressed laughter.

"You are impossible sometimes! Good thing you're cute!" I shouted at him.

He smiled real big and grabbed my hand and we locked up and got into Tammy to head to his parents' house. We pulled into the fancy place and parked and got out. I noticed Tony's car was there too. I thought it was odd, but maybe Pop had some business to take care of too. You never knew around there. We walked in and headed to the dining room. When I made it into the room it erupted with a simultaneous, "Congratulations!"

"What's all this for?" I asked in complete shock.

"Dee honey, we are here to celebrate you and your garage! We are so proud of you and happy that you are fulfilling your dreams," said Ma coming around the table to hug me.

I hugged her tightly and said, "Thank you Ma."

Pop spoke up, "I'm very proud of the way you've stepped up and got everything going. Anyone can start a business, but to get one running and doing well is something special. You've got it together Dee darlin.'"

"I couldn't have done it without the space. You and Trent went above and beyond for me and I can't thank you enough." I said holding back tears. I wish Sal could see this.

"You are thanking me. You're getting those cars fixed up for me and the charity ball will be a bigger hit than normal with an American Muscle car front and center." Pop said smiling.

"Kid tonight is about you and what you've overcome to get here. We want to be with you every step of the way and celebrate with you in your triumphs," said Tony smiling at me.

I thought I would never have a family and then here I was with a whole table full. I let the tears fall. Trent put his arms around me and pulled me close to him.

"Baby what are you crying for?" He asked sounding worried.

"I just realized what I've known for a while…I was alone for so long and now I have a whole family. I guess it just hit me how blessed I am. Thank you all. I love each of you and in a way this is more special, because we are a family that chose one another." I said smiling through my happy tears.

Dinner was wonderful. Ma made fried chicken, mashed potatoes, gravy, green beans, and corn. Of course, she made a cherry pie for dessert. The cherry was put on top when Ma presented me with a gift. I let Haley help me unwrap the small rectangular box to find a framed picture with Trent, Pop, Tony, and Me in it standing in front of my garage sign after it was put up. I smiled. This was the perfect gift. It would hang by Sal's picture. I hugged Ma and thanked her and then thanked her for everything again. My life finally felt whole.

That night, Trent made slow, passionate love to me. We had been like ravenous wolves since I let him have me. I wanted to experience everything and in every way and he was always happy to oblige, but he made deliberate love to me. It was slow and sweet and every little move felt so perfect. He loved me until the wee hours in the morning and I fell asleep facing him with my head on his chest.

Chapter 26

The months flew by with the garage up and running and new clients coming in daily. I did regular mechanic jobs like oil changes and repairs and then big full restoration jobs. I had four men hired that did the basic jobs while I worked on the big ones. Sometimes I would change oil or oversee a bigger fix. I got the Chevelle finished up two months before the ball. Pop was enamored with it. He sent out pictures to all the guests so they could see the main auction item. It was causing a lot of buzz.

Tony stopped by regularly to bring me pizza. He loved the shop and enjoyed working on cars too. He would step in and help me if I needed it while he was there. Trent stopped by most evenings and we would love each other in every way imaginable and go home and do it all again. I used the money from Sal's stuff to buy more equipment and tools and get some furthering education on business management. I opted to not go off to college with my new garage open and with Trent to warm our bed each night. I took online courses for business management.

Pop and Tony both taught me how to invest my money. The government was greedy I found and you couldn't just keep all your money in one place or you would get crazy taxed. I was grateful for both of them when it came to that. Tony became a regular a family meals too. My family was a bunch of crazies, but I wouldn't have it any other way.

I finished up Stephen's Porsche too. I painted it a cornflower blue and got her running like a top. Lilian made him come in with her car one day under the impression he needed to get the oil changed for her while she was at work. When in fact, I had gone and picked her up and she was waiting in the garage by his car with his favorite bottle of whiskey. The look on his face when he saw it, is what makes me love doing what I do. He looked like a kid on Christmas when he got in and started her up.

One month before the ball, Lilian called and said I couldn't go into work.

"Lilian, I can't just not go to work. The guys need me there," I said.

"Dee they can manage for one day and besides, I already called Tony. He will be there to oversee all the money exchanges. You know nothing bad will happen with him there," said Lilian with a smile in her voice I could hear.

"Fine. What time are you coming to get me?" I asked.

"Ma and I will be there in an hour," said Lilian.

The day was perfect. Ma and Lilian picked me up to go shopping for our formal dresses for the charity ball. I had never had a full on girls day like that. I never went to homecoming or prom or really anything that required really dressing up. We tried on dresses and shoes for hours giggling and doing impromptu fashion shows.

"Do you think this dress will give some in the middle?" Lilian asked as she looked in the mirror at the navy blue halter dress with beading around the top.

"I have no clue. Why are you asking that?" I asked her.

"That is an odd question, but it does look like a more giving material Lil. Why would you need it to…" Ma paused with understanding.

"I'm pregnant!" Lilian squealed as she wrapped her arms around both of us.

"Oh my gosh!! Yes! I'm so happy for you!" I shrieked back.

Ma was dabbing her eyes. "What a blessing another grandbaby. I can't wait."

Lilian did end up going with the navy dress, Ma got a very elegant one shoulder satin, red dress, and I of course found a deep green, sweetheart cut sparkly dress. It was formed fitting and straight down with a slit up passed my knee. We all felt in good in our choices. Ma explained that we had to be classy for this event. We all found shoes too. It was one of the best days I had ever experienced.

"Oh Dee, just wait until the day of. We get our nails, hair, and makeup done at the house. We don't let the guys see us until it's time to go and we have a limo pick us up. It's a big deal and so fun," said Ma.

I smiled looking forward to the day. I had never had any of that done. It seemed silly to get my nails done when I'd just mess them up working on cars, but I still looked forward to a day of pampering at Ma's. I loved these two women and Ma was the closest thing I had to a mom, since I was ten. I smiled.

"What color dress did you get Dee baby?" Trent asked me when I got home.

"Deep green. I love it. I've never had anything so fancy." I said smiling from ear to ear.

"Ok. I'll be sure my tux matches," said Trent wrapping me up in a hug.

"I want to take a bath," I said grinning up at the handsome man holding me in his arms.

He wiggled his eyebrows and swooped me up and carried me to the bathroom. We took a bath…Kinda. It was the best one I had ever had anyway. I loved how he knew my body and would always put my needs before his own. He was a giving lover and I tried to return that. I sat molded into him and thought how well I always fit into him.

Chapter 27

I woke up early the day of the charity ball. All I had to do was get pampered that day. The Chevelle was taken the day before to the casino to be set on a special platform. I didn't go. Tony and Trent took care of that, so I could keep working. Trent felt me stir.

"Good morning Baby," said Trent as he kissed my head.

"Morning. Sorry I woke you. I'm too excited to sleep anymore," I said going to get out of bed.

But, Trent pulled me back to him. He gently kissed my neck and began to rub me all over.

"Then, I should probably help you relax," whispered Trent in my ear as he nipped the lobe.

I giggled and gave into his musings. He had me on my side from behind, so we wouldn't kill each other with our morning breath. It was so good and I did fell a little more relaxed after we were both left panting. I got up and went to the bathroom and then went on to make us some coffee. Trent came in shortly after me and rummaged the fridge. He started to make some scrambled eggs and toast. I smiled watching him.

We ate at the bar like always, when the elevator door dinged and Lilian came hoping out.

"You're here early," I said smiling as she came towards us to get within reach and steal my toast.

"Hey that was mine," I said laughing.

"Well now it's your niece's or nephew's." Lilian said laughing. She continued, "I couldn't wait any longer to get out of the house and figured I'd come by here and get you so we don't have so many cars at Ma's."

"That sounds like a great idea. I'll go get dressed." I said kissing Trent on the cheek and moving towards our bedroom to get dressed.

"Make sure you wear a button up shirt so it'll be easy to get off and not mess your hair up," Lilian shouted with a mouthful of my eggs as I made it into my room.

I shook my head laughing. I grabbed one of Trent's button down shirts and a pair of yoga pants and slid them on.

"You girls have fun and don't get into any trouble. Give Ma my love," said Trent as he walked us to the elevator. He pulled me to him and kissed me.

"I'll see you later tonight." I breathed out.

He smiled and nodded.

Lilian told me the guys get ready at her house. I was so excited. We pulled into Ma's and she was waiting on us. She had decaf coffee waiting. She kept decaf for Lilian while she was preggers. We sat on the back porch and visited while we waited on the professionals to get there to do our nails, hair, and make up.

I sighed as I sat with my feet in a tub of warm water. So far this pampering thing was awesome. I had never had a pedicure and let's just say, it was fan-freaking-tastic. I got my toes and nails painted in a French tip. My hands looked pretty. My long brown hair was curled and partially swept back with blinged out pins. Ma got her hair in a regal updo. She just had two spirals at each ear hanging. Lilian had her hair braided back in a big loose braid and had rhinestones throughout her braid. We were coming together.

Haley came running in after our hair was done. She would get to go to the ball too for a while. Pop liked having his whole family there for the presentation. Haley got her little hair curled and braided back like her mommy's and she had a navy dress too. She was precious. Haley bounced with excitement when the makeup artist ran clean brushes across her face. Lilian let her have some sparkles on her eyes and she thought she was a real life princess.

Ma's make up was stunning. She had red lipstick on to match her dress and her eyes were lined in black and she looked amazing. She had on tear drop, dangling diamond earrings and tear drop diamond necklace. Lilian got a smokey eye and wore more of a burgundy lipstick. She had on a choker style pearl necklace and big pearl stud earrings. I had on a deep pink lipstick and my eyes were lined with a swept look and they had neutral tans and browns on my eyes that glittered. I looked stunning in the mirror. I had never been professionally done. Ma came up behind me and put her arms on my shoulders and smiled. She pulled out a little velvet jewelry box.

"This is for you Dee honey. Pop and I wanted to get you a little something to wear tonight with your dress." She said as she opened the box.

There was an emerald necklace, with the emerald in the middle surrounded by small diamonds and stud earrings to match. My breath caught in my throat. "You didn't have to do that. They are the most beautiful thing I've ever received. Ma, I don't know what to say besides thank you. You are the closest thing I have to a mom and I appreciate you and everything you do for me. Not to mention the man you raised." My voice started to crack.

"Oh hell no Dee. We are not crying and ruining our make up!" Shouted Lilian.

I laughed then and stilled my shaky breath. Ma put the necklace on me and I put the earrings in. They sparkled so bright. They would look so good with my dress. We dawned our beautiful dresses last and waited for our guys to get there. Haley was the most adorable thing ever. We all took selfies together and got the make-up artist to get pictures of all of us together. It was a special moment.

The doorbell rang. Ma looked up happily. "That's the driver. The boys are here. Let's go give them an eyeful!" Ma said walking towards the door.

We all headed for the door together. I could see the men standing outside the limo through the side glass window waiting on us. They looked so dashing. Trent was as usual gorgeous.

"Ready girls?" Ma asked as she put her hand on the doorknob.

"Yay!!" Screamed Haley.

We all laughed and Ma opened the door. She walked out first and straight into Pop's waiting arms. "My beautiful queen. You get more beautiful every day," said Pop kissing her on the cheek and shamelessly looking her up and down.

Lilian and Haley walked out next in their matching dresses. Stephen's face softened and he smiled so big. "My girls are gorgeous! Look at you my pretty princess," he said as a swirled Haley. Then, he grabbed Lilian by the hips and pulled her to him and whispered something in her ear that none of us could hear. She laughed and pecked his lips.

I came out last, pulling the door closed behind me. All eyes were on me and I was nervous. Trent gazed up at me and smiled. I smiled at him. I slowly walked down the steps and my leg would peak out of the slit with each step down. Trent met me at the bottom step. "Dee baby, you're beautiful every day, but damn baby. My breath was literally taken away by you. You are perfect," said Trent as he kissed me in front of everyone.

"Giorgie, let her up for air and don't mess up her make up for goodness sake," Ma said laughing.

"Sorry Ma. I just couldn't help it. Isn't she the most beautiful thing you've ever seen?" Trent asked.

"She is so beautiful." Ma agreed.

We rode in the limo to the casino. It was really cool. Haley loved the lights and we let her dance and sing in the middle. It took twenty minutes to get to the casino. I felt myself get nervous as we pulled in. I still had never gone into the casino. I wasn't sure if I really wanted to, given Brian's gambling problems. But this was Trentolini's and my father couldn't ruin this day for me.

Trent got out and held his hand out for me. I took it and stood up. Someone snapped a picture of all of us together. Then, another person was taking pictures of the couples as we walked in. I smiled for the picture as we walked into the casino. It was immaculate. There were chandeliers everywhere and flashing lights. The casino was closed to the general public tonight and guests were only admitted by invitation. Pop held this charity ball each year to support local charities that helped the homeless and underprivileged children of the area. All the high rollers were invited and many big business owners and family friends. The card tables were still up and running. All proceeds from those tables went to charity as well.

We made our way through the gambling parts to a big reception hall room that was decorated in golds and whites. The tables were covered in white table cloths with candles in the middle. Every seat was assigned. The meal was catered and it was fabulous. Then by the stage, was the candy apple red Chevelle with black stripes. She lit up the room. I took in a breath, when I noticed people staring at us as we walked through. Many people stopped Pop to say hi and have a few words. I noticed I was getting some crazy looks from young women there too.

I asked Lilian, "What's up with all these looks I'm getting?"

She laughed and said, "You took one of the most eligible bachelors off the market my flower and you look freaking hot."

I laughed. My sister was amazing. Trent held my hand tight in the crook of his arm and introduced me to key people. I got a lot of questions about Goon's Garage and managed to get some new clients. We sat at the head table in the front of the ballroom. We ate an amazing meal of filet mignon, scalloped potatoes, and green beans. Then it was time for dancing. Trent pulled me up from my chair and took me out onto the dance floor. He held me tight to him as we swirled around the floor. It was amazing. I felt like Cinderella.

Ten minutes before the car auction, we were called on stage with the rest of the family. Pop would give a small speech about the charities benefiting from the evening.

"Welcome friends and family. We are privileged to have you here with us tonight. My family and I thank you from the bottoms of our hearts for showing up to help our local residents in need and help those with no voice. I have been blessed abundantly and feel it's important to share that blessing with all those around me. From my beautiful family to yours, thank you and enjoy your evening. Without further ado, let me introduce Dee. She is the talented mechanic that restored our beautiful muscle car that is our auction item for the evening. Come on over here Dee darlin and tell these wonderful people about the car."

I went still. I had no idea I would have to speak. He waved for me to come to him and I did. I was nervous to say the least.

"Hi everyone. I'm so excited to be here. Let me tell you about this pretty Candy Apple red girl," I said motioning to the car. " She is a Chevy Chevelle SS 454. This is one of the most iconic muscle cars in America and she sports a whopping 450 horses under her beautiful hood. She has been completely restored and is up to any antique standard set. She would be an impressive car for shows or just to enjoy and pass down." I was saying as I heard my name.

"DEEEEEEE!!!" Haley shrieked in her cute baby voice as she came running toward me in her blue dress. I swooped down and grabbed her and smiled.

Haley was holding a tiny box in her little hands. I looked at it and then at her. "Haley girl, what do you have?" I asked.

I didn't notice Trent had made his way towards me as I was talking about the car. I looked to him to see him go down on one knee as I held Haley. My breath caught in my throat.

"DEEEE!!" Haley shrieked again handing me the box as Pop grabbed her from my arms.

I took the box and looked down to Trent on his knee in front of me. With shaky fingers I opened the box to see a ring and not just any ring, it was a huge princess cut diamond with two emeralds set on either side of it. My eyes started to glisten.

"Dee baby, I literally walked into your life and mine was changed forever. I love you more than I knew was even possible. We've shared so much already and I can't imagine experiencing anything else in my life without you by my side. It's been a crazy road to get to this place, but baby I wouldn't do this with anyone else. You make me proud every single day and happy every single day. Will you make my every day count and complete me and be my wife?" He asked looking through my eyes into my soul.

I let his words hit my heart and I let a single tear fall and nodded my head frantically yes and then shouted, "Yes!"

He stood up so fast and wrapped me up in a tight hug, swirled me around and then kissed me passionately in front of everyone. We stopped when we heard the hooping, hollering, and clapping. He sat me down and took the ring box from my hand and slipped the ring on my finger. I looked down at it and smiled up at him. My happiness was mirrored in his eyes. I grabbed his face and tenderly kissed him again. Pop and Ma were around us in a second hugging and kissing cheeks. It was a moment I would never forget as long as I lived.

"Let the auction begin and you all enjoy the rest of your evening. I know my growing family will," said Pop as he ushered us off the stage.

Tony was waiting for me at the steps of the stage. I had no clue he'd be there and he actually looked quite handsome in his suite.

"T-Daddy!" I shrieked as I plummeted into his open arms that were waiting for me.

"I'm so happy for you kid. You deserve all the happiness in the world," said Tony as he hugged me tightly.

He let me go and then shook Trent's hand and said, "It goes without saying, you better take good care of her or you deal with me. With that out of the way, come here man. I'm so happy for you both." He gave Trent a man hug where they pat each other on the back way too hard.

I laughed in complete delirium. Lilian grabbed me from behind and squeezed me tight.

"It's official! We are going to be sisters! I love you so much! It's been so hard to keep this secret!" She said smiling from ear to ear.

"I'm so lucky to gain you as my sister! You've been the best since the first day I met you! And Haley coming up to me..My heart is mush," I said with a soft smile.

"That was all Giorgie's planning. He put a lot of thought into this. He loves you so much and the rest of us love you too." Lilian said, hugging me again.

Trent took me to the side and we snuggled up for a quiet moment alone in an alcove away from everyone.

"You really surprised me in the best way possible. I'm one lucky chick to have a hot guy like you love me so perfectly. I love you so much Trent," I said melting into him again.

"Dee baby, I'm the lucky one. You are the best thing to ever happen to me. I will love you every day and never let you feel alone again. I'm yours baby," said Trent kissing the top of my head.

"And I'm yours forever," I said closing my eyes and relishing the moment.

The car brought in $250,000! I was so surprised. Apparently these people had plenty of money and I found out they could use it as a tax write off. Trent and I went mingling around. We were congratulated so many times and people were smiling at us. We walked through the card tables about to sneak off to go home, when I spotted her.

Chapter 28

I halted in my step, pulling Trent to a stop with me. He looked confused. "Dee what is it?" He asked.

"It's her," I whispered.

"It's who?" He asked still confused.

I looked at the woman who looked exactly like me, but older and a little heavier. Trent followed my gaze. I heard him intake a deep breath. She hadn't seen me yet. I wasn't sure what to do. Surely she saw me on stage with my new family.

She looked up and her eyes locked on mine.

It was a moment of complete recognition. Her eyes went soft and she gave a tight lipped smile. She was standing at a black jack table. "How fitting?" I thought as I looked her over. I would have thought she would be as far away from gambling as possible. Then it hit me, where I was, who I was with, and what was still part of my life. I turned to run out the door, but Trent still had a hold on my arm and I couldn't run.

"Don't run Dee baby. You don't have to talk to her. Let's just go home." He said.

I nodded, my mouth dry, and my heart starting to literally hurt. We turned and walked out of the door. When Trent opened the door of the limo, I heard her call from behind me, "Dee Anne! Wait!"

I froze. Trent stiffened next to me. She made it to me and put a hand on my shoulder. "Can I please talk to you?" She asked.

"I don't know that we have much to say Anne," I spat out a little more harshly than I expected to.

She visibly flinched. "I deserve that Dee. There's a lot you don't know though. I'm happy for you sweetheart. Seems you caught you a real good one here," Anne said nodding towards Trent.

I looked at her. "I didn't catch him. I wasn't after his money or his name. He found me actually. He showed me what it's like to be put first for once in my life. He showed me what love is and what family means. Ma, his mom, has been a mother to me. I'm nothing like you or Brian." I said firmly.

"Dee baby, let's just go home. You don't have to do this right now. Anne this is supposed to be a happy day for both of us." Trent spoke up.

"Dee Anne," her voice shook and I finally took a moment to really look at the woman who brought me into this world.

She was wearing a skimpy skin tight, sequin, black dress that her cleavage was bursting out of. She had on dark make up and a lot of it. Her hair was big and everywhere. Her eyes were sad. I looked to see the dress was barely long enough to cover her behind. I kept looking at her.

"What are you doing her Anne?" I asked.

She let a little cry leave her throat and shakily answered, "There's so much you don't know. I wouldn't have left you if there was any other way. You have to know that. I think of you every single day. Not one day goes by that I don't pray for you or hope you're in a good place. At least I know that prayer has been answered. I can't say much more..I..um…"

"What do you mean you can't say much more? What don't I know? You can't claim all that stuff and leave me wondering still," I said getting more angry.

"Annie, what the hell you doing out here?" A grizzly voiced man hollered from the door.

I watched Anne slowly close her eyes, regain her composure, and say, "I was just congratulating the beautiful couple Sugar. Aren't they just perfect?"

"Uh yeah. Congrats Trentolini. Got you a looker for sure. Come on Annie. There's still fun to be had," said the man gruffly.

She looked at me one last time and turned and walked in, leaving me behind once more. I saw Tony at the opposite door, watching everything. Tony was always my shadow. I noticed he kept an eye on me all the time. I looked up to him and he looked at me and nodded. There was something I needed to know and Tony had answers or I knew he would find them.

Trent and I got into the limo. I fell into his arms and cried. This should be the happiest day of my life and it was just pummeled into a crazy direction by the appearance of my mother. Trent just held me. When, we got home, he kissed my face and walked me inside. I sat on the edge of our bed, with my shoulders sagging. He walked over to me and kneeled in front of me and slipped my heels off my feet and rubbed them watching my face. He picked up my right foot and pressed his lips to my leg just above my ankle. It sent a shiver up my back. Trent ran his hands up my legs and then wrapped his arms around my waist and rested his head in my lap. I rubbed his head and wrapped my other arm around him.

I looked at the handsome man in my lap. I thought about how he planned the perfect proposal and how he just held me and let me feel what I needed to. I picked his head up and looked directly into his beautiful green eyes and said, "Giorgio Moe Trentolini Jr. I love you with all I have and I can't wait to be your wife. I'm sorry I let her get to me. I'm not going to let anything ruin this night. I want you naked right now."

He gave me his crooked grin and said, "Yes ma'am. I aim to please."

We slowly helped each other undress. He kissed every inch of my body and I in turn did the same. He kissed my hand right on my ring. I smiled at him. I took him in as I laid back on the bed and parted my legs for him. He slowly stroked himself as he looked at me laid out ready to take him. He crawled up my body and settled himself in between my legs. He kissed me passionately and I let my hands roam his back down to his bare ass that I squeezed and pushed to me. He smiled on my lips and situated himself and gave me all of him. We made love with more passion than most people would believe. Our mouths always on one another, hands taking in the other, and bodies never coming unconnected, even when switching positions. It was a beautiful moment in time. We were both breathing hard and sweating when, he gave me his release on a whispered, "I love you," into my mouth. I took his mouth and his release and held on.

We stayed tangled up together until we got out of bed the next morning. Anything that had bothered me the night before was lost in my love to him. I didn't have to gamble just because his father owned a casino. I didn't have to take part in any of that. I wasn't just arm candy for him at some table. I was his partner and he respected me and my work. I smiled at him as he sat in one of the barstools sipping his coffee while I made us omelets. I was just in his white dress shirt from the night before.

"Dee baby, it's taking all I got, not to have you right now. You're killing me in my shirt cooking for me. I want to…." He was saying as I cut him off.

"Shh. I know what you want to do, but we need food first," I said laughing.

He gave me puppy dog eyes and I gave him a pouty lip. I shook my head and went back to making swiss cheese and mushroom omelets. Before I had the spatula ready to flip the omelet, I felt Trent wrap his arms around my waist and press into me.

"Trent, I'm making us breakfast. Stop it," I said heated.

"I know you don't want me to stop. Let me have an appetizer before breakfast," he said letting his hand roam to my intimate areas and going down to his knees behind me.

"Trent," I breathed out as his hands rubbed up my ass and pushed his white dress shirt up.

"Mmm. This is what I want," said Trent as he buried his face in between my legs.

I let out a whimper, but he was right I didn't want him to stop. With my hands shaking, I got the omelet out of the pan and onto a plate, turned the stove off, and turned to see my fiancé on his knees before me. My eyes went hot. I pushed him down on the floor and took him right there on the white, cold, hard tile. My knees were pounding, but it didn't matter. All that mattered was getting this man to loose himself in me.

We were both giggling as we ate the cold omelet. He kissed my mouth after I took a bite and I said, "Gross. My mouth is full."

He laughed and said, "I just ate you for breakfast and your worried about me pecking you with a bite of omelet in your mouth?"

I nodded and said, "I can see your point Mr. Trentolini."

"Good soon to be Mrs. Trentolini," said Trent smiling at me.

I loved to hear that. My phone rang and Trent answered for me.

"Hey Tony. What's up?" He asked.

"You need to come by now?" Trent asked.

"Ok. We will be here. Come on," said Trent hanging up and looking at me.

"What's Tony need to come over for today? I'm sure he understands we are still celebrating this big rock you put on my finger," I said with my eyebrows raised.

"He said it's about your mom. It's something we both need to know," said Trent looking a little stressed.

I just nodded and felt like a rock had hit bottom in my stomach.

Thirty minutes later, the elevator dinged with our visitor. Tony entered the room in his black combat boots, faded jeans, and a white t-shirt on. I went to the elevator to greet him.

"Hey T-Daddy. Is everything ok?" I asked, feeling nervous.

"Kid, I think will be. I never put two and two together. Annie, your mom, that guy she's with…He's bad news. I don't know the whole story Dee. You'd have to get that from your mother. His name is Arthur Linchino. He's got a whole mob family. They get into some real shady stuff and unfortunately kid, I know shady," Tony said looking uncomfortable.

"What are you trying to say Tony?" asked Trent.

"I'm saying that they don't need to find out Annie is Dee's mother. If they feel there's any family connection, they will manipulate it to their benefit. They will threaten to hurt Annie for Dee to give them money or information on your family Trent. They are bad. They are power hungry. I'm sure your father only invites them to stuff to keep the peace and because they like to flaunt their money to look more powerful than they are." Tony said looking Trent directly in the eye.

"T-Daddy, what are we supposed to do then? What about my mother?" I asked feeling sick to my stomach.

"Kid, I don't know the story on your mom. I know Brian got himself in over his more times than I can count. If he got himself in with the Linchino's, your mom was most likely collateral damage. I will continue to dig and see what I can find, but I have to do it quietly. It may take time. In the meantime, I will go to work with you every day to keep an eye out. I've been talking with my employer, I'm getting old and I am ready to retire. I will do that soon and just be your private security detail and only go in for him when it's something urgent. Trent you need to get your dad on board too. Until I can figure out what's the deal with Annie, I can't be sure that Dee is safe," Tony said on a long breath.

"Ok. Pop will do anything for Dee. He loves her as his own already. I'll see what I can find out too. I have some resources with PI stuff," Trent said looking at Tony.

I felt numb. Was I seriously still not safe? I thought after getting away from Brian and having my new family, I would be safe. I had harbored such bitter feeling towards my mother all these years. Was she just collateral damage too? How bad was it? Or did she choose that? My head was spinning.

"Dee did you hear me?" Tony asked.

"What? I'm sorry. I've got a lot running through my head," I said.

"I know kid. We are going to keep you safe. You need to make sure you have either Trent or myself with you whenever you leave, until we get this all sorted out and any threat neutralized," said Tony.

"Neutralized?" I asked.

"Don't ask kid," said Tony looking over my face. "I'd do anything to keep you safe. You've really become a daughter to me and I took you on to protect a long time ago. I couldn't save my little girl, but I be damned if I let someone hurt you while I'm here."

I hugged him tight. "I'm sorry I asked. I know. I know you love me. Which brings me to an important question T-Daddy."

He looked at me worried I was going to ask something he couldn't answer.

I asked, "Seeing how you're my T-Daddy, I need someone to walk me down the aisle. Would you give me away on my wedding day?"

Tony's eyes warmed and tears filled them and he said, "I'd love nothing more than to walk my little girl down the aisle. I promised Sal I'd be there for you if he couldn't. I do love ya kid."

Tony put his hand on my cheek and nodded. This was a type of closure for us both, but now I wondered how uncertain my future was with this mob family lingering. I had questions about my mother. I had questions about my father. And I had a wedding to plan and a business to run.

Chapter 29

My life continued almost as normal. Trent drove me to the shop every morning and Tony would be there waiting for me at the door. Trent threw himself into investigating my mother. He worked tirelessly trying to make sure I was safe. Pop would make several stops during the week at the shop to take me to lunch.

It was to show that I was an important part of the family and under his protection, in case anyone was watching. Even though it was a screwed up time, it was a special time. I really got to bond with Pop and T-Daddy. I got to know them on a level, I never had with Brian.

My garage was thriving, especially after the charity ball. I had a lot of high rollers using me for their everyday car maintenance and new projects. Old muscle cars were a popular commodity among the business men. I was making so much money, that I was investing it in a boutique for the garage. I had Lilian figuring it all out. We were going to make Goon's Garage shirts and other merchandise. It would be making money and advertising all at once. Life was good. Ma was helping me plan my wedding. We decided to have it at their house under the trees. She was so excited.

I had gotten so used to life being so good, that I forgot to be ready for the shoe to drop. Arthur Linchino came rolling into the garage one day in his Mercedes. I was waxing an old Camaro when he walked in. I recognized him immediately and I saw Tony exchange some words with him at the door. Tony walked him over to me and I sat my wax rag down and smiled.

"Mr. Linchino right?" I asked pleasantly.

"Arthur please and I hope it's not too bold of me to call you Dee?" He asked in return.

"Not at all. That's my name anyhow. How can I help you today?" I asked smiling and giving Tony a side glance.

"Well, Dee, I'm looking into getting an old car for fun. I was hoping you could help find something," He said smiling at me.

I nodded and said, "I actually have a 1970 Plymouth Barrcuda all ready to go. I'm not sure what you really want, but she's pretty awesome. She's completely restored and is up to factory specs. She is painted Sublime Green, like a lime green. She's a fast one too. She's got a 340 V8, 3 speed automatic transmission, and coup body style."

"Dee, I've got to be honest, I'm not really sure what any of that means. Does it look bad ass?" Arthur asked.

I laughed and said, "She's all muscle. Why don't you come look at her and see if she's something you're interested in and if not we can figure out what your style is."

"Sounds perfect. I have mechanics for a reason. I'm illiterate when it comes to cars. I took up other hobbies," he said trailing off looking at Tony.

Tony stood still.

"Follow me," I said leading both men to the back of the garage where I kept finished cars.

I took him right to the Barracuda and he whistled. "Damn this car is sexy. How much do you want?" Arthur asked smiling at the car.

"I'll have to give Pop a call and see right quick. I don't outright own this one," I said moving to head to my office.

"Pop?" Questioned Arthur.

"Oh sorry Giorgio, my soon to be father in law. I forget sometimes. He bought several old cars for me to restore, like the Chevelle at the charity ball. It's an investment for him and we both get something out of it," I said smiling.

"I see. So if I stumbled across some old cars, we could maybe work a deal to where we both make some money?" Asked Arthur raising his eyebrows.

"I'm always up for making money. Tony oversees a lot of my outside deals like that," I said lying through my teeth and nodding towards Tony.

Tony smiled and nodded his approval at me. I was doing well. Arthur needed to know I didn't work alone. I stepped away to head to my office to hear Arthur ask, "So what you got going on now Tony? This is a little slow for your normal style. What's this girl mean to you?"

I didn't stick around to listen. I went to the office and called Pop.

"Dee darlin, everything ok?" He asked as soon as he picked up my call.

"Yes I'm fine. Arthur Linchino is here and he wants to buy the Barracuda. I wanted to see what you wanted to sell it for," I said.

"Oh I see. Text me over the total you have in parts and labor and I'll head that way to personally handle this transaction," Pop said sounding very businesslike.

"Yes sir. See you soon," I said as I hung up and got my paperwork ready to text over.

"Good news," I said walking back to the two men still standing by the car.

They both looked up.

"Giorgio is on his way over. He said he wanted to be here to make a deal in person," I said.

Arthur raised his eyebrows, "Oh yeah? Cool."

I nodded and smiled.

"Oh hey, I never told you congratulations on your engagement. I know Annie did, but I was doing good at the blackjack table and I just never got the chance. I guess you were ready to get home to celebrate. Trent is a good guy," said Arthur and it seemed like he was genuine.

I smiled and said, "Thanks. He is the best. I'm one lucky girl and I get an awesome family too."

"So how do you and Tony know each other? I know Tony has never been close with Giorgio," asked Arthur.

Tony answered, "I've known her since she was a kid. She worked for a friend of mine in his garage. I took her under my wing after he suddenly died. Dee is like a kid to me."

Arthur smiled and said, "Wow Dee, you really are a lucky woman to have such prominent men in your life. Tony is a good guy too no matter what anyone says."

"I have to say Arthur, I don't know much about you. Are you a good man?" I asked feeling bold.

Tony blanched. Oops I may have messed up.

Arthur smiled even bigger. "You are a bold one aren't you. I can see why Trent would be drawn to you. I'm a good guy to certain people I care about. You and I are going to be friends Dee. I can tell. Anyone brassy enough to call me out, I like."

I laughed softly, "I have to say I've heard I have grit more than once. Ok guys, I have some cars to work on. Giorgio will be here soon and you can iron out the details on the car. It was nice to officially meet you Arthur."

"Nice to meet you Dee," he said coolly.

I turned and walked off and heard him say to Tony, "Dee is amazing. Trent is a lucky man."

I felt my skin crawl, but I didn't feel threatened by Arthur. Maybe that was dumb on my part.

Giorgio made it and they made a deal and he drove off in the Sublime green Barracuda. Giorgio walked over to me as I worked on an old Oldsmobile.

"You made the right decision by calling me down Dee darlin. I'm proud of you. Arthur sees that you are in my family. Don't put your guard down though." Pop said grabbing my arm.

I nodded and smiled at him. I didn't like feeling like I needed to watch my back again.

That evening after Tony dropped me off at home, I walked into the kitchen to find Trent cooking dinner. I smiled at him and went and wrapped my arms around his waist and let my head rest on his back while he stirred spaghetti sauce.

"Mmm. Smells good," I said into Trent's back.

"Me or the food?" He asked chuckling.

"Both," I said planting a hard kiss on his back.

He turned from the stove and wrapped me up in his arms and kissed my forehead. "I love you," he said.

I smiled and returned it, "I love you too."

"I found out some stuff today Dee. About your mother. We are going to run into her tomorrow at a coffee shop she goes to every week. Hopefully you can get some answers on our accidental run in," said Trent as he air quoted accidental.

I laughed and said, "ok then."

The next morning, I called Tony and filled him in. He would run the shop for me while I was out for the morning. I put on a light blue t-shirt dress and white sandals. Trent wore jeans and a collared shirt. He was impossibly gorgeous just in jeans. Trent drove, so we were in Tammy. We made it to a little whole in the wall coffee shop. The coffee was fantastic. It was a neat find in such a big place.

Then, I saw her walk in. She was alone and in jeans and t-shirt. She had on big sunglasses. When she took them off, I saw the black eye. I inhaled deeply and Trent followed my gaze and when he saw her, his face went hard. I stared at her until she felt my stare and turned to see me. She immediately looked down as if she was embarrassed to meet my eyes.

Anne went and ordered her a French vanilla latte and waited at the counter for her drink. I could tell she wanted to split, but there was no way I was going to let that happen. I got up and walked over to the counter and didn't turn to look at her.

I just started to speak staring straight ahead, "You said there was so much I didn't know. I want to know. I need to know. Arthur showed up at my garage yesterday and judging by your eye, he's not a very nice man. Am I in danger?"

Anne's shoulders slumped, "I don't think so. I never told him you were my daughter, but he has his ways to find out things. He's the reason I don't have worse than a black eye."

"None of that makes any sense. Please just tell me everything. I don't understand why you left me with Brian. Do you know how hard my life was? I had to get a job at thirteen." I said closing my eyes remembering feeling so alone.

"I didn't want to leave you. It was the only way I could keep you safe. Your father was always getting himself into trouble with his gambling and his debts. I was trying to find a way out. We didn't have anywhere to go, but I had managed to buy two bus tickets and was just going to leave with you and figure it out. My parents were both dead. All I had was you and Brian. You were at school, when someone broke through the living room door. I was terrified. I didn't know who he was. He was screaming at me and asking for Brian. I of course, didn't know where he was either," Anne said her voice starting to fade.

"What happened?" I asked feeling the tears well up in my eyes.

"He asked if I had any money. I of course didn't. I said all I had was fifty bucks and two bus tickets. He asked me why I had two tickets. I told him I was going to sell the other for whatever I could get and get out of there. I never got the chance. Your father showed up finally and the guy roughed him up pretty good right in front of me. I didn't even scream for him or ask him to stop punching him. When the guy realized your dad was a lost cause, he said, "I'm taking your wife as payment. She was going to leave you anyway and now when you think of me and how much you owe, you can imagine your wife naked under me." I was in shock. I had no choice. I went with him and never mentioned you or they would have come after you too," she said letting the tears fall.

"Mom, I didn't know. Brian just said you left us. I just thought you couldn't handle being with him anymore..." I trailed off letting it all sink in.

"Well, I paid your father's debt off unwillingly. I was sold night after night to whoever would pay for me. After two years of that, the debt was paid off. I wanted to leave but I was scared to lead anyone back to you and by that time, Arthur decided he wanted to keep me anyway. There was no escaping him. He buys me nice things and doesn't sell my body anymore. Dee he can't know you're my daughter though. If I can't do anything right, I cannot tell him about you," she said shaking.

"Mom...I'm so sorry. I've been so mad at you all these years. I don't know what to say. I don't want you to live that life anymore. Let me take you home. I can help you," I said grabbing her hand.

She pulled her hand away from me quickly and hissed, "No one can know. No one. I love you so much Dee, that I will walk away from you again. That's how much I love you." And she turned and walked out.

Chapter 30

I sat in our kitchen numb. I couldn't believe Brian let my mom go through that and never tried to help her. I had since filled in Trent, Tony, and Giorgio. I couldn't imagine the hell my mom went through and she did it to protect me. My childhood had been hell, but it was my own life. I wasn't under some man's thumb having to do unthinkable things. I shuddered.

Trent wrapped his arms me. I had been in a state since the news. He was holding me tight. I needed him so badly to just hold me together. When I closed my eyes, I saw my mother's sad face. She had lost years with me for my father's cowardice and bad habits. I wasn't going to lose any more time with her. I called Tony to come over.

"Dee what's this about?" He asked me.

"I'm going to get my mom back," I said firmly.

"Dee this is tricky. If Arthur finds out she's your mother, it could get messy. He could expect to be part of the family. I'm not sure about this. I understand you want to help her, especially after finding out what she's been through…."Tony was saying.

I cut him off, "I have plenty of money. Can I buy her off from him?"

"I don't know Dee. He seems to like her. He's not just going to want to let her go." Tony said.

"Will you try? Even mobsters have family," I said nodding.

"I'll see what I can do," said Tony.

I hugged his neck and whispered, "Thank you."

The next week I was a wreck wondering if Tony had enough pull. I was worried sick my mother would be stuck there. I didn't know what to do. I just knew I had to do something and save her. She didn't deserve anymore of that.

Tony came walking in the garage and right into my office, where Trent and I were taking lunch.

"Dee I've got good news." Tony said smiling at me.

I couldn't help but smile, "Oh yeah?"

"Arthur and I have been in conversation all week about Annie. I told him that I'm retiring and I could use some help around my house and I wanted a live in maid. I asked him if I could take Annie of his hands and hire her. He agreed. He said he was moving on anyway and that he would give her to me as a retirement gift. He seems extra happy I won't be knocking heads anymore," said Tony.

"Well that's great! Mom will be safe and away from him," I said feeling happy.

"Now Dee look, she's going to have to live with me and she still can't go around saying she's your mom. Arthur would take that badly." Tony said.

"I'll take whatever I can get. Arthur knows you're like a father to me and maybe in time he'll think I see Anne as a mother, but in a different way. Thank you for all that you did. I know you had to pull some of your goon strings and I appreciate it so much," I said looking up to him.

Tony left to go get my mom and Trent wrapped me up in his arms. I kissed him feverishly.

"Dee Baby, you have people in your garage," he said slowing the kiss.

I got out of his arms and locked my office door.

"Good thing my office door locks and the windows are covered. Come here Trent. I want to happy bang you," I said giggling.

"Happy bang?" Trent questioned with his eyebrows raised.

I nodded and went closer to him, grabbing him through his pants. He groaned and I smiled, "Yes happy bang."

Trent left to go to the grocery store. I would have mom and Tony over for dinner after she got settled in at Tony's. I sent him with a list. Tony was going to get my mom and Trent would be back to get me at closing time. Life was good.

I gave out the last paycheck and saw my employees off. I went to shut down my computer, when I heard my front door open.

"Sorry we are closing up shop," I shouted from my office.

My heart stopped when I saw who walked through my door.

Chapter 31

I stiffened as Brian closed the distance to my office. I pulled out my phone and hollered, "Un uh. Put your phone down." He said pulling out a gun.

My breath stilled and my eyes keyed in on the hand gun. I set my phone down on my desk. He came and picked it up and looked at it and said, "Oh how sweet. Your screensaver is you and Sal."

I didn't say anything. I sat still, just watching him. He looked at me and screamed, "Don't you want to know why I'm here?"

I shook my head no. "I don't care why you're here. Obviously you've got yourself in another bind somewhere. I know the truth about mom now. Did you know the woman you supposedly loved enough to marry had to sell her body to cover your debt? Did you know?" I screamed.

He looked shocked at me and scratched his temple with the barrel of the gun. "Of course I knew. How else would they get the money. That was the best thing she ever did for me."

"Oh really? Not giving you a daughter? Funny I thought it would be me," I said through clenched teeth.

"You? You don't even care about me. It was only Sal for you," he spat out.

"It was because he was there. You were never there for me. You left all the time and I had to raise myself. I had to figure out how to pay bills and feed myself. I had a big scary guy waiting for me at home one night looking for you!" I shouted.

Brian started shaking. He pointed the gun right at me and said, "Well if you're the best thing your mother ever gave to me, let's see if that holds true."

"What do you want Brian?" I asked.

"Finally she wants to know," He screamed. He continued, "I want all your money. All of it. I know you're worth a lot now. You're marrying Trentolini's kid. Classic. You will be fine without this." He threw his hands around and waved his gun.

"People will know something is wrong if I get rid of my shop. This is my dream and Sal worked hard to make sure I'd have it. I won't give you my shop. Money fine, but never my shop." I said.

"You will give me everything. You owe me that. I gave you life and kept a roof over your head. You and your mom were never happy with me. Look at you now…You left me too…" He trailed off. He wasn't in his right mind.

"No one ever left you. You weren't even there to leave. Mom had no choice and I had no choice either. There was nothing there for me and I got caught up in your problems too. You know I met Trent because he was looking for you. Looking for the twenty grand his dad loaned you to help you out. You put me in the wolf's den and I became part of the pack. Don't get upset because I know how to adapt and survive." I said standing up now.

I saw a man walking up to the shop door. "Oh God, Trent. He can't come in. I can lose him and I don't want him to see me get shot," was all I could think.

"You want to shoot me, shoot me! You will not get a dime from me! You don't deserve it! Shoot me and leave everyone I love alone!" I screamed at the top of my lungs.

"Maybe I should just shoot you and get it over with. I'm your next of kin. I'd get it all anyway," He said snarling at me.

I smiled. "That's what you think."

My world went black, I heard the shot, but I didn't feel it and I vaguely heard a man screaming and then felt hands I didn't know on my face. My heart was slowing down. My last thought was, "Trent I love you."

Chapter 32

"Arghhh!" I wasn't dead, but I felt like I might wish that. I hurt so badly. I came to in an ambulance.

"It's ok ma'am. We are to take care of you. You will be ok. Hang in there," a paramedic told me. He continued, "You lost consciousness. You've been shot."

That much I remember. I whispered, "Brian Rice. Did it."

"The cops have him ma'am. You are safe now." He replied.

"AHHH! This freaking hurts so bad. My fiancé, Trent. Where is he?" I panted out.

"We are giving you meds for the pain. Your fiancé will meet us at the hospital. Try to relax," said the paramedic guy.

That was the last thing I heard, before my world, yet again, went black.

I woke up to hear beeping and feeling my hand being held. My throat was so dry. I needed water. I opened my eyes to see Trent slumped over by my bed, holding my hand. I touched his head and croaked out, "Hey."

He quickly picked his head up and looked at me searching my face. He stood up quickly and pressed his lips on mine and ran into the hall and called for my doctor.

"Water," I managed to get out.

"In a minute baby. Let the doctor come in first and ok it," he said squeezing my hand.

The doctor came in and told me I was lucky and that I'd make a full recovery. I was given water and that was glorious. I looked to Trent who was just watching me.

"Dee baby, I'm so sorry I wasn't there. I should've been there. If you would of...I couldn't live without you...."He trailed off with tears filling his eyes.

"But I didn't and I'm here. He would of shot you if you'd been there. What happened Trent?" I asked.

"Arthur showed up as Brian was pulling the trigger and he hit him. That's why the bullet went into your shoulder instead of your heart. He was coming by to talk to you. He knows that Anne is your mom. He wanted to hash it all out with you and tell you his side of the story. Anyhow, he saw Brian and he reacted. He saved your life. He said the last thing you said was, "I love you Trent." Baby I love you so damn much." He let the tears fall now.

I reached my good arm up and wiped his tears away with my hand. "Trent, it's ok. I'm going to be ok. You still have me. Where is Brian now?" I asked.

"The police have him. He's got a long list of chargers lined up against him," he said.

I nodded. "I'll be safe now with him gone. What about Arthur? What was he after?" I asked.

"Actually, nothing. He had put two and two together after seeing you at the shop. He figured Tony was asking for you. He respects you and says he doesn't want to go to war with us or Tony. Apparently, he is hoping he can do some car business with you. I told him as long as he posed no threat to you, we would work something out. He agreed and said your mom took care of any debt Brian owed him and that he was glad to get to you in time. He was relieved you didn't die. It shook him up to see a woman shot. He's no saint and what he did to your mom is despicable, but I'm glad he made it to you in time to change the path of that bullet. Maybe your mom can pursue her own justice later. We are going to have a long happy life. Tony and you mom are still here too. They just went to get a coffee break. They'll be so happy to see you awake. My family is waiting on the call. Ma is cooking lasagna. She said you need a good meal as soon as you wake." Trent filled me all in.

I smiled. I had my family. If I knew it would have only taken me gambling my life to my father, I'd placed that bet a long time ago.

Epilogue-One year later

I waited just inside the house, in my white formed fitting wedding dress. It was lace with a sweetheart line and a long train. Tony was right by my side. Lilian handed me my bouquet that was full of white roses and many different kinds of greenery. I had on my emerald necklace and earrings. I was excited. My life was all working together for the good. We had just opened a second Goon's Garage that T-Daddy and Mom ran. They had gotten close. I was happy they were finding happiness with each other. They hadn't come out and said they were a couple, but they totally were. She had lived with him since getting out of Arthur's hold. Mom told her story to FBI investigators and got a lot of bad guys behind bars, including Arthur.

Lilian's second child was a son. He was the cutest little boy ever and was just a few months old now. I asked Stephen to hold him up during our ceremony, because he was my nephew just as my little flower girl, Haley was my niece and they were an important part of my big day. Lilian and Stephen were the only ones we asked to stand for us. Ma, Pop, and Mom sat on the very front row.  Ma and Pop went above and beyond for the wedding. They had more lights strung up through trees and a canopy of lights for our dance floor and eating area. Of course Ma made lasagna for our food. Our wedding was small and intimate. Only our family and closest of friends were invited. I couldn't wait to marry the man that had knocked me over the head and saved my life all in one night.

I tightened my grip on Tony's arm. He looked to me. I said, "T-Daddy, I know you wish you could be walking your little girl down the aisle and this day has to be bittersweet for you. Thank you for being here for me and showing up. You're walking us both down the aisle today."

I picked up a small picture of his daughter that I had stuffed in the middle of my bouquet and showed him. I wanted her to be a part of this day and I hoped she knew I appreciated her sharing her dad with me.

Tony's eyes filled with tears and he let one fall. I reached up and brushed it off and said, "I love you T-Daddy. We are both proud to have you stand for us."

Tony said with a sweet smile, "I love you too kid. More than you know and I am walking my tough, little girl down the aisle. Let's get you married."

When the preacher asked, "Who gives this woman to be married?", Tony answered, "Her mother and I." I squeezed his hand tight. He was still thinking of someone besides himself and after he kissed my cheek and leaned in to put my hand in Trent's, he said, "And even though I've grown to love ya, I'll still break your legs if you hurt her."

Trent laughed and said, "I'd have it no other way."

He looked at me with his green eyes and our life was just beginning. It got even better when we opened our wedding gifts and found a brand new office chair from Lilian. No one understood why she got us this, but we did and I laughed so hard. It was so good to have a full family. I looked over everyone there for us. They were a bunch of goons, but they were my goons. I was now a married woman and had my dreams all laid out before me. I knew Sal would be proud and I knew he would have approved of Goon's

Garage. Names always meant something to him and the garage belonged not only to me, but to every goon in my life, good and bad. They all had shaped me into the person I was today. I smiled to myself and Trent looked at me with a knowing smile. We had been through a lot together, but our journey was just pulling out into the Fastlane .